THE HIDDEN EVIL

Deep in Sheena's heart something stirred. It was
not really a memory but something less explicable, more obscure. It was a re-echo, perhaps,
of something she had felt and which at the time
had not been able to put into words. What was
it? She could not explain it to herself.

Then quite suddenly, like a light coming
through the window, she knew that all through
the terror and horror and fear of what she had
experienced she had known that she was not
going to die. She had known unmistakably and
yet absolutely that she would live and be saved.

And she had known, although until this moment she had not been sure of it, that the person
who would save her would be the Duc.

Arrow Books by Barbara Cartland

Autobiography

I Search for Rainbows
We Danced All Night

Polly: the Story of My Wonderful Mother
Josephine Empress of France

Romantic Novels

1	*Sweet Punishment*	38	*Love on the Run*
2	*The Black Panther*	39	*Theft of a Heart*
3	*Stolen Halo*	40	*The Enchanted Waltz*
4	*Open Wings*	41	*The Kiss of the Devil*
5	*The Leaping Flame*	42	*The Captive Heart*
6	*To Mend a Heart*	43	*The Coin of Love*
7	*Towards the Stars*	44	*Stars in my Heart*
8	*Armour Against Love*	45	*Sweet Adventure*
9	*Out of Reach*	46	*The Golden Gondola*
10	*The Hidden Heart*	47	*Love in Hiding*
11	*Against the Stream*	48	*The Smuggled Heart*
12	*Again This Rapture*	49	*Love Under Fire*
13	*The Dream Within*	50	*Messenger of Love*
14	*Where is Love?*	51	*The Wings of Love*
15	*No Heart is Free*	52	*The Hidden Evil*
16	*A Hazard of Hearts*	53	*The Fire of Love*
17	*The Enchanted Moment*	54	*The Unpredictable Bride*
18	*A Duel of Hearts*	55	*Love Holds the Cards*
19	*The Knave of Hearts*	56	*A Virgin in Paris*
20	*The Little Pretender*	57	*Love to the Rescue*
21	*A Ghost in Monte Carlo*	58	*Love is Contraband*
22	*Love is an Eagle*	59	*The Enchanting Evil*
23	*Love is the Enemy*	60	*The Unknown Heart*
24	*Cupid Rides Pillion*	61	*The Reluctant Bride*
25	*Love Me For Ever*	62	*A Halo for the Devil*
26	*Elizabethan Lover*	63	*The Secret Fear*
27	*Desire of the Heart*	64	*The Irresistible Buck*
28	*Love is Mine*	65	*The Odious Duke*
29	*The Passionate Pilgrim*	66	*The Pretty Horsebreakers*
30	*Blue Heather*	67	*The Daring Deception*
31	*Wings on my Heart*	68	*The Audacious Adventuress*
32	*The Kiss of Paris*	69	*Lessons in Love*
33	*Love Forbidden*	70	*The Complacent Wife*
34	*Danger by the Nile*	71	*The Little Adventure*
35	*Lights of Love*	72	*Journey to Paradise*
36	*A Light to the Heart*	73	*The Wicked Marquis*
37	*Love is Dangerous*	74	*A Heart is Broken*

Barbara Cartland

THE HIDDEN EVIL

ARROW BOOKS

ARROW BOOKS LTD
3 Fitzroy Square, London W1

An imprint of the Hutchinson Publishing Group

London Melbourne Sydney Auckland
Wellington Johannesburg Cape Town
and agencies throughout the world

First published by
Hutchinson & Co (*Publishers*) Ltd 1963
Arrow edition 1966
Second impression 1970
Third impression 1973
This edition 1975

Made and printed in Great Britain
by The Anchor Press Ltd
Tiptree, Essex

ISBN 0 09 908120 2

1

'Pour le nom de Dieu shut the door!' a man exclaimed angrily from the fireplace, as the sea wind swept boisterously into the room, whistling down the backs of the four gallants sitting with their legs stretched out before the pot-room fire.

'I must apologise, Messieurs, if I intrude,' a voice replied sarcastically.

The four young men sprang hastily to their feet. Framed in the doorway of the low-ceilinged inn was a resplendent figure in a velvet doublet flashing with jewels, a plumed hat set jauntily on the side of a dark head, and high boots, which strangely enough seemed not to have encountered any of the mud which made the inn yard almost a quagmire.

'Your . . . your Grace!' one of the young men stammered. 'We did not expect to see you here.'

'I did not expect to be here myself,' the Duc de Salvoire answered, closing the door behind him and crossing towards them as he drew off his embroidered gloves.

'You too are meeting the ship from Scotland?' one of the young men hazarded respectfully.

The Duc shook his head.

'Nothing so adventurous,' he said. 'I have been staying at Anet and I am on my way to join the King in Paris. However, Her Grace the Duchesse de Valentinois requested me to carry a message for her to the Convent of The Poor Sisters who live in this God-forsaken place—only the Lord they worship so devoutly can know why!'

Unconsciously, from force of habit, the Duc took the

best chair and seated himself in the most comfortable place by the fireside. A vague gesture of his hand, wearing a huge emerald ring, indicated that the others might be seated, and they settled themselves, but without the comfortable, relaxed abandon with which they had been enjoying the warmth of the fire when His Grace arrived. Now, a little tense and on edge, they sat politely in their chairs, their faces turned towards him as they waited for him to speak.

They were four of the most staid and sensible young men of the Court, the Duc noted, and guessed it was the Duchesse who had had the good sense to choose such a band for the mission with which they had been entrusted.

'She never fails,' he thought with a little smile, and wondered what other King's mistress had the wisdom and the good sense or the statesmanship of Diane de Poitiers, who for ten years had virtually been the Queen of France.

As if the trend of his thoughts somehow communicated itself to the young men sitting round him, one of them asked:

'Were you sorry to leave Anet, Monsieur?'

The Duc smiled and the twist of his lips seemed for a moment to remove the tiredness and also the boredom from his eyes.

'One is always happy at Anet,' he said. 'The Duchesse and the King have built together a house of love which is without its equal in the whole world.'

Just for a moment his listeners looked surprised. They were not used to hearing such warmth in the Duc's voice. He was known to be bitter and cynical. Crossed in love, so the story went, when he was but a boy of seventeen, he had vowed never to let his heart run away with him again. In fact he was known on more than one occasion to say: 'I have no heart, only a brain which is far more reliable.'

Almost as if he regretted having spoken so warmly and in such a manner, the Duc's next question was spoken in the hard, bored tones that habitually characterised him.

'You speak of meeting a ship from Scotland?' he enquired. 'Or was that merely an excuse to hide some nefarious smuggling across the Channel? I am told that the ports of Brittany are filled with English gold.'

One of the young men laughed.

'There is nothing you do not hear, is there, your Grace? It is true that smuggling is on the increase; but it is all in the French favour, and so who are we to discourage a good customer, however unsavoury he may seem when he is not putting his hand in his pocket?'

'You have not answered His Grace's question, Gustave,' another gallant interposed. 'We are here, your Grace, to meet the new *gouvernante* to the young Queen of Scots.'

The Duc raised his eyebrows.

'Indeed! I was not aware that we had to send to Scotland for one. Can it be that there is no one of education and intelligence in France?'

'I agree,' Comte Gustave de Cloude said quickly. 'It is almost an insult that we should have to send abroad to what by all accounts must be a barren and barbarous land for someone to instruct the future bride of the Dauphin. But 'tis said that the little Queen herself took such a distaste for Madame de Paroy that she insisted on her dismissal.'

'Insisted?' the Duc asked softly. 'A child of thirteen— or is it fourteen?—years!'

'That is what they say, your Grace,' the Comte replied.

The Duc smiled.

'A will of iron at that age. Ah, well, perhaps France can use it! She should be a good mate for the young Dauphin.'

There was a moment's silence. Everyone in the room was thinking the same thing—that the weak, fragile boy with his strange blood disease would need a strong, resolute wife if he was to rule the greatest, richest and most civilised country in the world.

Then with a change of mood the Duc broke the silence almost harshly.

'For all that I consider it an insult,' he said. 'Must we have some pock-marked, long-nosed, carrot-headed Scotswoman spoiling the look of our palaces? A plague on her!

7

Let us hope that the ship from Scotland has foundered and we shall be saved from the new *gouvernante* from the north.'

As he finished speaking, his voice echoing round the small, black-beamed room, there was a gust of air which seemed almost to lift the chairs from under the listeners, and a young voice, cold, icy and yet clear as a mountain stream, said:

'I regret to inform you, Monsieur, that your wish has not been granted. The ship has not foundered but has docked safely.'

There was a moment of stupefaction and five faces turned towards the speaker. Then the wind seemed literally to b'ow her into the room and some unseen hand from outside pulled the creaking door to and left her amongst them.

Hastily, with a sudden exclamation, the Comte Gustave de Cloude sprang to his feet.

'The ship has docked? We were not told!' he exclaimed. 'We should have been on the quay! What has happened to the visitors from Scotland?'

'Most of them have retired to their rooms,' the girl answered.

She was, indeed, but a girl. About seventeen or eighteen, the Duc decided, rising slowly and with dignity when the other men present were already on their feet.

He looked at her and met a pair of vivid blue eyes staring into his with undisguised hostility. She was very small— no big-boned Scotswoman here—but the little curls, which had been whipped by the wind round her white forehead, were undoubtedly red-gold in colour.

Never, the Duc thought in astonishment, had he seen skin that had such a crystalline purity about it so that it appeared almost transparent.

'The party has . . . has retired!' the young Comte was stammering. 'This is disastrous, Ma'mselle. My friends and I were to have met them and welcomed them to France on behalf of the King.'

8

The girl turned her eyes from the Duc towards the Comte.

'There was no one on the quay,' she said, 'so we walked to the inn.'

'And Mistress Sheena McCraggan,' the Comte questioned, 'is she upstairs? Could you not persuade her to see me for one moment that I might proffer my apologies and deliver to her personally the messages that I carry on behalf of His Majesty?'

'You may deliver them if I can come nearer the fire,' the girl replied. 'My feet are soaked through. I had no idea that France could be so muddy.'

'But . . . but, Ma'mselle, you cannot be . . .'

'I am Mistress Sheena McCraggan,' the girl said with a little touch of dignity which was almost incongruous because she was so tiny.

There was an audible gasp and then a silence which was broken by the Duc saying suavely:

'Mistress McCraggan, may I welcome you to France? If we seem somewhat at a loss, it is merely because we expected someone older.'

'I heard what you expected, Monsieur,' Sheena said severely, turning her face away from his so that he could only see the tip of her tiny, straight nose and the clear line of her little chin.

The young gallants could scarcely prevent a smile showing on their lips. They were so used to the Duc's harsh tongue that it was a strange experience to see him rebuffed, especially by a girl who seemed scarcely out of the schoolroom.

They made way for Sheena to come to the fire. She held out her hands towards the blaze and then with a gesture completely simple and without a trace of coquetry in it she undid the ribbons of her wet bonnet and pulled it from her head.

Just for a moment it seemed as if the sun had come out in the dingy room. Contrary to any woman's hair they had ever seen before, Sheena's head was covered with tiny, dancing curls, golden red, which sparkled in the firelight and seemed to make a halo that framed her little pointed face and oval forehead.

'Ma'mselle, allow me . . .'

The young men sprang eagerly to bring forward a chair, to put a cushion into the back of it, to take from her her cloak, gloves and bonnet.

'A glass of wine, Ma'mselle? You will need it after your journey.'

'Thank you, but I would rather have chocolate if that is possible.'

'It shall be procured immediately.'

One of the gallants hurried from the room; another knelt down and drew her small, buckled shoes from her feet.

'Your shoes are soaking,' he said. 'I will find a chambermaid and get them dried unless it is possible to unpack a part of your luggage and find another pair.'

'There will be time for them to be dried, I think,' Sheena answered. 'Father Hamish, who has accompanied me, will not be able to travel for a few hours. He was terribly seasick and so was his manservant and my lady's maid. We must give them a little chance to rest. They have had no sleep for days.'

'But you, Ma'mselle, you did not mind such a tempestuous sea?'

'I enjoyed it,' Sheena answered. 'My home is on the sea and I am used to being out in all weathers, sailing or fishing with my father. But I was not expecting it to be so cold.'

She held her feet out towards the blazing fire. They were very small, beautifully shaped feet, but clad in thick knitted stockings. And now, almost for the first time, they realised how plainly and almost poorly dressed she was.

She wore a gown of homespun wool, discreetly modest, with no jewellery and undecorated by silk or satin or any of the frills and furbelows that were commonplace amongst

10

the great ladies of France that men noticed them only where they did not exist.

'Tell us about the voyage, Ma'mselle,' someone hazarded as if he was interrupting an awkward silence.

'There is really nothing to tell,' Sheena replied, 'except that the sea was very rough from the first moment when we left Inverness. Nevertheless, the ship brought us here safely. It was a fine ship, built in Scotland as only the Scots can build ships.'

Now there was a defiant note in her voice. She looked across the hearth to where the Duc was sitting watching her, a faint smile on his lips which seemed to her almost a sneer.

She thought to herself that she had never seen a young man's face that should have been handsome so ruined by lines of cynicism and boredom. He was the type of man she most disliked, she thought. The type she dreaded to meet at Courts and in the company of kings. The type which had made her exclaim to her father:

'I will not go! What use would I be in a palace surrounded by clever people who have nothing to do but to seek amusement?'

'You should be grateful for the opportunity,' her father had replied.

'The opportunity for what?' she asked. 'Oh, I am willing enough to serve our Queen, you know that. But is it likely that she will listen to me when there are so many other people to attract her attention?'

'Her Majesty is living in a sink of iniquity, in a place where the devil reigns and revels in unbridled dalliance,' her father had replied. 'I knew it when it was decided to send her to France; but what else could we do with Scotland being ravished by the English, the crops burned and soldiers searching everywhere for the babe?'

He paused and Sheena knew from the pain in his voice and the expression in his eyes that he was thinking of all the cruelties and horrors suffered by the farmers and peasants who had taken no part in the war against England

11

but who were killed, their women violated and their lands destroyed.

'We were forced to send her,' he went on, his voice harsh and almost raw at the memory. 'And we believed that those we chose to be near her would behave with decency . . .'

He stopped abruptly and walked away from Sheena to stand with his back to her looking out of the narrow latticed windows of the castle.

' 'Tis not right,' he muttered, 'that I should talk of such things with you.'

Sheena knew all too well to what he referred. There was not a family in the length and breadth of Scotland who, loyal to the young Queen, had not been appalled and horrified when the news came that Lady Fleming, governess to Her Majesty, had attracted the notice of Henri II.

'She is to bear his child! '

Sheena could still hear the whisper that was passed from mouth to mouth and ear to ear.

'Mother of the King's bastard—and she was the one whom we sent to France to watch over and instruct our own little Queen.'

News travelled slowly; and almost before the first shock of learning what was happening had reached the North, they heard that Lady Fleming had returned to Scotland and given birth to a bouncing boy.

'What of the Queen? Who is with her? From whom is she receiving instruction?'

The information that Lady Fleming's place had been taken by Madame de Paroy, a Frenchwoman, was followed several months later by the news that the young Queen had taken a dislike to her new instructress.

'She has a violent temper,' the Queen's subjects were told. 'It is born in her.'

This, however, was no consolation, and the wiser amongst the Queen's advisers in Scotland concentrated on the more important decision as to who should replace Lady Fleming.

Strangely enough, it was one of the older men who had the idea of sending to France not a strict governess but someone who could be a companion to the young Queen.

'I do not think it is instruction that Her Majesty needs,' he said gruffly. 'There are plenty who will give her that. I believe it is someone in whom she can confide; someone with good, sound common sense who will show her that the vices of the French Court are not such as can be tolerated by decent people. What is the point in sending an old person? The young never listen to the old.'

It was an idea that had not occurred to anyone before, but each one of those seated in Council realised that it was a solution to their difficulties. Lady Fleming had placed them in the unfortunate position of having to apologise for their own morals.

Easy enough to censure the French. Easy enough to point a finger of scorn at a King who ruled France with his mistress and practically ignored his wife save for the fact that she produced a child regularly every nine months. It was difficult, however, to be so censorious now that the chosen protector of the young Queen, a lady of importance, of good family and a Scot, had let them all down by her adulterous and despicable behaviour.

They all realised the problem of trying to replace Lady Fleming. Should they send a woman so ugly and unattractive that the King would not look at her, there was every chance that the young Queen, already by all accounts spoilt and impetuous, would find her unattractive too and demand her dismissal as she was demanding that of the Frenchwoman.

But to send somebody young would offend no one—someone young enough to talk and laugh with a fourteen-year-old and someone who was also young enough, praise Heaven, that the King, licentious monster that he might be, would treat her only as a child.

'You have a daughter, Sir Euan,' the elders had said to Sheena's father, and although he fought against the idea of dispatching his only daughter across the seas to a land

13

in which he believed Satan reigned unchecked, he found it hard, indeed impossible, to resist the arguments with which the elders tried to persuade him.

It was far more difficult, he found, to persuade Sheena.

'You do not understand, Papa,' she said. 'I shall be the laughing-stock of the Court. I have no clothes, no polished manners, no sophisticated wit. If Mamma were alive it would be different. She would know what I was to expect and would be able to warn me.'

'If your mother were alive,' she heard her father say almost beneath his breath, and saw the sudden clenching of his hands until the knuckles were white.

Her mother had been dead for ten years and yet the hurt was still there; the emptiness and the loneliness without her, while the fragrance of her scent and her personality still lingered in the grey solitude of the Castle.

'I cannot go, Papa! I cannot!'

'You must!'

He shouted the words at her and she knew it was because he was upset at the thought of losing her.

He crossed the room to her side and when she expected him to be fierce he was suddenly tender.

'The McCraggans have always been loyal to the Royal cause, Sheena,' he said. 'We cannot fail Her Majesty now. Many of us have given their lives—and God knows I am prepared to give my own whenever it may be required of me—but it is not just broad-swords and claymores that can settle something like this. This is more subtle, more difficult to understand. We are dealing with serpents and we have, ourselves, to acquire the guile of serpents.'

He dropped his voice.

'You will go to France, Sheena, and not only to do what you can for the young Queen, but also to find out how far France is prepared to support Mary Stuart as the rightful Queen of England.'

Sheena was suddenly very still.

'You are asking me to be a spy, Papa?'

'I am asking you to serve your country as every man of

our clan is willing to do—not by dying, but by trying to learn the truth.'

'But, Papa, surely the King of France will support our Queen. He knows that when Queen Mary dies it is Mary Stuart who should succeed to the Throne.'

'Does he believe it? And if he does, what is he prepared to do about it?' Sir Evan enquired. 'We are so far away, chi'd. How are we to know what he is thinking? How are we to know what help he will give us? And without France are we strong enough to beat England?'

Sheena felt herself shudder. It seemed to her then as if her father was voicing the fear and anxiety which beset the whole of Scotland. They surely knew that their cause was right, that Mary Stuart was the true Queen of Scotland and heir presumptive to the throne of England. But had they the arms, the money and, above all, the men to set her in her rightful place?

The thought of what she must do had lain heavy on Sheena's heart all through the journey. And now, as she looked round the room at the rich garments and flashing jewels of the Frenchmen hovering around her near the fire, she felt a sudden scorn.

Could they be anything but sops and effeminate, these men dressed in silks and satins and velvets, wearing jewels and a greater profusion of feathers and laces and ribbons than any Scotswoman would have worn on her most elaborate evening gown.

A comely chambermaid in a mob-cap came through the door carrying a steaming cup of chocolate which she set down beside Sheena, talking all the while in a dialect which was hard to understand.

'The priest, God bless his soul, is better. With a little cognac in his stomach the sickness has subsided. But your maid is still in tears, Madame, and says not if the King himself asked her could she put a foot to the ground, for 'tis still swirling under her as if the waves had come with her from the sea itself.'

'Will you please give her something to eat and say that

15

I shall hope to leave for Paris within the hour,' Sheena said.

It was the voice of authority. The chambermaid looked mildly surprised.

'I will tell her, Madame, but I doubt we'll get her on her feet, poor soul. She's vomited until there's nothing left to vomit and still her stomach is queasy.'

'I shall be grateful if you will convey my message,' Sheena said, and turning to the gentlemen she added: 'I hope, Messieurs, you will permit me to travel as soon as possible. I have a deep anxiety to reach Her Majesty and start my duties.'

'You are in a great hurry,' the Duc remarked. 'Would you not be wiser to rest here tonight? The place is poor but clean.'

'In Scotland, Monsieur,' Sheena said, straightening her back and looking at him full in the face for the first time since their exchange of hostilities, 'we put duty first and comfort a very long way behind.'

His lips twisted at the corners and she had the impression that she had made no more impact upon his sensibilities than if she had been a fly brushing itself against his velvet coat.

'Very commendable, Ma'mselle,' he said. 'Very commendable indeed. We must all admire your persistence and, of course, your devotion to duty.'

The sarcasm in his voice was so obvious that Sheena could not help but retort. Her fiery Scottish temper, never very well controlled, flashed for a moment like lightning across her eyes. Then she said in a tone as icy as that which she had used when she first came into the room:

'I think, Monsieur, that I shall fare best without your praise, for words from a twisted tongue are often dangerous to those who have serious and important work to do.'

Even as she spoke Sheena was half frightened at the challenge of her voice as well as of her words. In that moment her eyes met the Duc's and they stared at each other, the shabbily dressed girl with her dishevelled curls and her wet feet held out to the flames, and the man with his magnificent attire, flashing jewels and tired, cynical eyes.

It was war between them and they both knew it. War— inescapable, deadly and pitiless. A war in which one or the other must ultimately be the victor.

As if the other people present realised that something momentous was taking place, no one spoke. Then very slowly the Duc rose to his feet. For one moment he stood towering above Sheena, his head almost seemed to touch the ceiling.

Then he swept her a magnificent and exaggerated Court bow.

'Your servant, Ma'mselle,' he said. 'We shall meet in Paris.'

Still in silence he turned and walked from the room. The door closed behind him.

Sheena did not turn her head. She knew something strong, tempestuous and frightening had gone, leaving the room curiously empty. She suddenly felt very tired and very alone.

2

They were nearing Paris. Sheena bent forward in the coach to stare about her with wide eyes at the fine châteaux which they passed from time to time and the cultivated fields which lay on either side of the road as far as the eye could see.

Every mile that she travelled nearer to her destination made her realise her own inadequacy and the poverty of her appearance. She had not expected anything so luxurious or so comfortable as the coach which had been sent by the King to convey her from the little fishing port to Paris.

'We shall travel at great speed,' one of the gentlemen in

her escort had said to her; and after the rough roads in Scotland and the uncomfortable, hard coaches which had been her lot until now, Sheena could hardly believe it possible that horses could move so quickly or that she could lie back in such comfort against the padded cushions.

Her knees were covered with a rug of velvet lined with fur, and she thought wryly that it was incongruous that anything so delicate should be required to cover the coarseness of her gown.

She had felt so elegant when she left Scotland, for she had sat up half the night struggling with the old seamstress of the village to achieve what she imagined was an exceedingly fashionable wardrobe and worthy of the girl who had the privilege of waiting upon the Queen of Scotland. Now she felt that she looked nothing but a laughing-stock.

She could only compare her own possessions with those of the young gallants who accompanied her. As they rode on either side of the carriage, the silver accoutrements on their horses' harness glittered in the pale sunshine, their cloaks of velvet and satin billowed out behind them in the wind, and the ostrich feathers on their caps waved gracefully with every movement they made.

'I must look like a servant girl,' Sheena whispered to herself.

Then defiantly her little chin went up. Her blood was as good as theirs if not better, and the blood of Scotland was being shed at this very moment in the defence of her Queen.

Yet at seventeen it is hard to be resolute in the face not of adversity but of plenty. Sheena did not miss the way that at every inn at which they stopped the ostlers ran forward to change the horses, the innkeeper bowed low to the ground and the maidservants curtsied.

She was travelling in a Royal coach; she was under the protection of the King of France; therefore she was treated with a respect which was akin to reverence. It was something she had never known before in her whole short life in the barren castle in Perthshire.

The priest who had been her companion on the sea voyage had gone no further. He was journeying to Calais to join the English garrison there and to bring the homesick, bored troops news of their homeland.

Sheena and Maggie were alone—and Maggie, with her high cheek-bones, sharp, angular features and bright inquisitive eyes, was somehow something strong and familiar to which she could cling almost desperately in her apprehension of what lay ahead.

'Dinna fach yerself, ma bairn,' Maggie said, sensing what Sheena was thinking. 'Ye're as good as they are, nay—better. All they've got that ye have'na is money—and what has money brought them but laziness and corruption?'

'You cannot say that, Maggie,' Sheena replied, laughing, although she felt more like bursting into tears. 'We have not seen the Court. We must not judge until we have been there. The King has been very kind to us. Look at this wonderful coach and our escort. He could do no more if we were the little Queen herself and not just a troublesome addition to her household.'

Maggie snorted.

'Fine feathers!' she said. 'Men dressed up like women in their silks and satins and diamonds. I'd rather have a mon who can wear a plaid and knows how to wield a claymore. Pah! 'Tis doubtful I am if any of this crowd will fight for Her Majesty.'

'Hush, Maggie! Hush!' Sheena said.

'They'll no' understand us,' Maggie said scornfully.

'Look at that house,' Sheena breathed in admiration, as they swept past a great château standing back from the road in a garden in which there were ornamental lakes and fountains playing. There were swans, black and white, swimming on the silver water and it seemed to Sheena as if the whole scene was out of some fairy-tale.

She thought a little wistfully of her own home, the ramparts crumbling from old age, the doors and staircases sadly

19

in need of repair, the rooms furnished shabbily and without comfort.

Everything here in France appeared to have been newly painted. Even the villages through which they passed seemed clean and the people thriving and prosperous. She had heard many tales from the elders in Scotland of the extravagance of the French monarchs—how Francis I, father of the present King, had taxed his people unmercifully to pay for his war with Spain and for the band of innumerable mistresses who travelled with him wherever he went.

She could hear her uncle, the Earl of Lybster, denouncing him with a violence which made his voice echo round the room.

'A dissolute and corrupt man,' he had boomed, 'who died from a disease which came from his excesses. A King who was a disgrace to the Monarchy wherever he might reign.'

Sheena had only been a child at the time and her uncle had not realised that, sitting in the window, half hidden by a tattered velvet curtain, she was listening to him.

'You must concede, Sir, that he was at least a patron of the arts,' someone remarked.

'Arts!' Lord Lybster shouted. 'What does art lead to but licentiousness? To men such as rule over France it means statues and pictures of naked women; it means debauchery where there should be discipline and lassitude where there should be strength of purpose.'

Sheena had wondered why they should feel so violently about a King who had lived so many miles away and was long since dead. And then they had gone on to speak of Henri II, son of Francis, who now ruled France and to whose protection they had entrusted the Queen of Scotland.

It was amazing, she thought, the stories and the gossip which managed to drift back across the sea. Mary Stuart had enchanted the French King! She had sung to him and had recited a poem that had almost moved him to tears! A tale that was most often repeated was that when Mary first curtsied to Henri II at Saint Germaine when she was not yet six years old, he had exclaimed:

'The most perfect child I have ever seen!'

It was compliments of that sort that fed the loyalty of the rough Scotsmen and kept them eternally on the defensive against the ever encroaching onslaughts of the English.

'Tell Her Majesty that we are fighting for her by day and by night,' Sheena's father—Sir Euan McGraggan—had said as he kissed his daughter farewell. 'Make her understand how loyal the c'ansmen are, how much she means to us all, that we live for her return.'

Sheena had been moved at the simplicity of his words. She had known only too well that they were nothing but the truth and that the men waving goodbye as her ship moved away from the windswept quay sent with her a part of their hearts.

She had been utterly convinced at that moment that it was right that she should go. Mary Stuart must not be allowed to forget those who strove for her against almost overwhelming odds.

She thought it would be easy to tell the Queen stories of the heroism and courage and unquenchable bravery which drove the Scots into battle against far superior forces and which made them accept, with an almost unbelievable fortitude, the burning and laying waste of their lands and crops.

Now, nearing Paris, she began to be afraid. What had this sunlit, rich land in common with the great barren moors, the burns, swamps and dales where a man could march for days, if not weeks, and not meet another soul with whom he could pass the time of day?

'Maggie, I am frightened,' Sheena said impulsively.

'Shame on ye! Ye're nothing of the sort!' Maggie retorted tartly.

She did not meet Sheena's eyes and they both knew the feeling of uncertainty and fear of what lay ahead.

'They are kind gentlemen,' Maggie said almost gently,

'despite their fanciful garments. They will show us the way right to the King's door if nothing else.'

'If only we had some money with which we could buy different clothes,' Sheena breathed almost beneath her breath.

'They must take us as they find us,' Maggie retorted. 'The men who are fighting for Her Majesty are doing it often in bare feet and without a piece of cloth to cover their shoulders. Let her remember that. Make her understand the sacrifices that are being made not only by the men themselves but by their wives and bairns.'

'I will try,' Sheena said humbly.

She cheered herself up with the thought that Mary Stuart was nearly three years younger than she was herself; only a child, whereas she had come to womanhood. It should not be hard to instruct a child into the truth.

Despite such comforting assurances her hands were cold, her fingers trembling a little, as she laid them on the arm of Comte Gustave de Cloude as he helped her to alight at the Palace.

She had expected it to be regal, but she had not expected so many servants, such a bustle of liveried flunkeys, of major-domos and sentries, besides numerous personages who had apparently little to do but stand around, waiting and staring.

Sheena was allowed only a few moments to tidy herself after the journey and then without being allowed to change her travelling gown she was ushered straight into the presence of the King.

She was ready to hate and despise him. The stories of his liaison with Diane de Poitiers had lost little in the telling when they crossed the sea—his neglect of the Queen; the fact that he ordered the initials 'D' and 'H' to be entwined as a monogram and carved on all his palaces. These stories had made her father snort with indignation.

Sheena had not known quite what she expected the King to look like. Whatever the image she had preconceived it was certainly nothing like the heavy, mournful features of the dark-haired man who looked at her with melancholy eyes.

'Mistress Sheena McCraggan, Your Majesty!' she heard a voice say, and swept to the ground in a deep curtsy.

'Mistress McCraggan, we have been looking forward to your arrival,' the King said.

'I thank you, Sire.'

Sheena was surprised to hear her own voice, clear and apparently unafraid. She rose to stand before him, small and straight-backed in her crumpled, homespun gown, her head held high so that the evening sun coming in from the window behind the King's head glittered on the red-gold curls she had tried to straighten into unaccustomed neat-ness on either side of her cheeks.

'You had a good journey, Ma'mselle?'

'The sea was very rough, Sire.'

The King nodded, as if he had expected the sea to be rough, and then he said:

'You speak French extremely well.'

'My grandmother was French, Sire.'

'Yes, yes, I have not forgotten. Jeanne de Bourget; one of the oldest families in France. You have good blood in your veins, Mistress McCraggan.'

'I am proud of my Scottish blood, too, Sire.'

'Yes, yes, of course.'

Henri was obviously bored with the conversation. He looked round the audience chamber as if at a loss, won-dering what he should say or what he should do, or per-haps seeking guidance.

And then the door opened and his face was suddenly transformed. The look of melancholy vanished, the air of uncertainty was changed. He moved forward quickly. Sheena turned her head. The most beautiful woman she had ever seen in her life was coming into the room.

She was not young and yet there was something so youth-ful in her movements that it was as if spring itself had sud-denly emerged to cast away the darkness of winter. She was dressed in white with touches of black and yet the purity of the colour only served to show the whiteness of her skin.

'She is like a camellia,' Sheena thought, surprised at her own sense of poetry.

The lady in black and white sank to the ground before the King.

'Forgive me, Sire, if I am late,' she said.

He bent forward to raise her hand to his lips.

'You know that every hour that you are away from me seems like eternity,' he murmured.

Only those nearest to him could hear what he said but everyone could see the adoration in his eyes, the pleading of his lips, the change that had come over him since the opening of the door.

Still holding the hand he had kissed with his lips he turned towards Sheena.

'Mistress McCraggan has arrived,' he said. 'She has had a rough voyage, but she is young enough to survive it.'

The beautiful woman smi'ed at Sheena, a smile so warm, so embracing, that Sheena felt some of the tension go from her.

'We are so glad you are here, Mistress McCraggan,' the lady said, and then as Sheena curtsied she added: 'The little Queen has been looking forward to seeing you. It will be nice for her to have news of Scotland and her people who must miss her sorely.'

She could have said nothing which would have gone straighter to Sheena's heart.

'Indeed, Madame, in Scotland our thoughts are only of the time when the Queen will return to us.'

'That is how it should be,' the King said a little ponderously. 'And now, Mistress McCraggan, the Duchesse de Valentinois will take you to your mistress.'

Sheena felt herself stiffen. So this was Diane de Poitiers, Duchesse de Valentinois, the Grande Sénéchale, who had bewitched the King and seduced him so that he had eyes for no one else.

She had known, she thought, the moment the Duchesse

24

had entered the room, but somehow she had been so bemused, so taken aback by her beauty and her charm, that she had for a moment forgotten the scandal and the gossip, the spite and the condemnation, that she had listened to in Scotland about this very woman.

She had thought somehow that she would never see her. That the King would keep her in some secret place where only he visited her. She had not thought ...

'The Queen has been in my charge, you know,' the Duchesse was saying quietly. 'I have been supervising her education. Her Majesty is a very promising pupil. You will be surprised at how talented she is and how quickly her education has progressed in the last few years.'

Sheena found herself unable to answer. What would her father and the other statesmen say if they knew? To be brought up by a courtesan, by a woman they had all declaimed as a prostitute, lower than those who followed in the wake of the Army or who paraded the streets of Edinburgh at night.

Diane de Poitiers! A witch they had called her. And yet now, with incredible graciousness, she was leading the way down the corridors of the Palace.

'Heaven knows,' Sheena thought, 'what the little Queen has been taught under such auspices.'

Had Her Majesty's education been one of witchcraft and guile, of how to blind a man's eyes so that he would forget his duty and his honour simply so that he could receive a smile from those red lips?

'You must be very tired after your journey,' the Duchesse was saying, and it seemed to Sheena that her voice was almost hypnotic it was so easy to be deceived by it.

'I have had a room prepared for you near to that of your Queen. You will have much to talk about in the next few days and after you have met I suggest that you go upstairs and have a sleep. If you are not too tired, we shall welcome you at dinner. There will be dancing afterwards,

25

but if you prefer to do so, sleep until morning and start the day fresh.'

'I have no need of rest,' Sheena said grimly.

Already she was beginning to see the magnitude of the task which lay ahead of her. How could she alone undo the harm which must have been done to the little Queen by this evil woman?

Perhaps she had been kept shut up with her alone, having no one decent and respectable around her to whom she could turn to learn the truth or to weigh in the balance all the wrong and twisted things they were putting before her under the guise of education.

'Your Queen is very busy at the moment,' the Duchesse was saying. 'She has been learning her part for the play she and the Royal children are to act before the King next week. It will be a very gay evening. Perhaps you will be able to help with the final details.'

Sheena felt herself shiver. Play-acting! What would her father say to that? She could see his hands raised in horror, hear the anger in his voice if she told him that Mary Stuart was to strut the boards and to perform as if she were a common actor. The audience might consist of a King and his Court, but the wrong was still there.

They had reached the end of a passage hung with wonderful pictures and carpeted so that it seemed as if one's feet walked upon velvet. They turned and another great corridor lay ahead of them.

'This part of the Palace,' the Duchesse was saying, 'is given over to the Royal children. Some of them are very young, as you may know, but the Dauphin and Queen Mary are almost the same age and they have many interests in common. There are many other companions for your Queen as well. Thirty-seven children of the nobility of our land share her studies and her sports.'

'Thirty-seven!'

Sheena ejaculated the words in absolute astonishment.

The Duchesse smiled her beautiful, glorious smile which

revealed the whiteness of her teeth and made her exquisite eyes twinkle a little.

'Yes, thirty-seven. I hope you did not think we left our little Scottish visitor without interests or amusements.'

'No . . . no, of course not,' Sheena stammered.

'At first her four little friends—the four Marys who came with her from Scotland—were sent away; but only so that she should learn French. It is so difficult to learn any language when one is talking one's own all the time. But now they are constantly with her, although just at the moment they are still in the country for a special rout which they had promised to attend some time ago. Only Mary Stuart has come back to Paris especially to greet you.'

'That is gracious of her,' Sheena said quickly.

'And here I think we shall find her,' the Duchesse said.

The door she indicated was flung open for them by a flunkey resplendent in gold lace. Sheena eagerly followed the Duchesse into the room.

It seemed to her that all this had been a wearisome preparation for the moment when she would see her own Queen, when she would start the work she had come to do and for which she had travelled so many miles.

And then as the chandeliers, pale-grey walls, carpet covered in roses, and great hangings of exquisite embroidery swam before her eyes in a kaleidoscope of colour and movement and steadied into being only a frame for the person who stood waiting at the far end of the salon, Sheena saw Mary Stuart.

She had expected a child. She saw instead a young woman who appeared far older than herself. Her hair was that strange liquid gold of which the poets had written since the beginning of time. It was not unlike Sheena's own hair and yet there the resemblance between them ended.

Mary Stuart was taller than Sheena and her full, oval face had a beauty that was almost classical in its conception. There was no flaw to be found in it and perhaps because it was so cool, so flawless, so smooth and clear-cut, the face was a little lacking in expression.

And yet Mary Stuart's beauty lay in her skin, in her hands, long, slim and pale as snow, and in the way she held herself. There was nothing that was not beautiful about her, and yet somehow Sheena felt a little stab at her heart as if she had expected too much and found something lacking.

Her feet carried her forward without her being conscious that she moved. Then, as she reached the Queen of Scotland and sank down before her in a curtsy that was not on'y a greeting but a reverence, the Queen spoke.

'So you are Sheena McCraggan!' she said. 'I thought I should remember you, but I do not.'

She sounded disappointed and Sheena said hastily:

'It is many, many years ago, Your Majesty. You were little more than a babe.'

'I thought you had dark hair,' Mary Stuart said, a little petulantly. 'I must have been thinking of someone else.'

Sheena rose from her curtsy. Never had she expected her first conversation with the Queen of Scotland to be like this. She had planned so often the things she would say, the greetings she would bring her; and now she could only stand tongue-tied, something cold and unhappy crushing at her heart.

'I wonder who it was I found myself thinking about?' Mary Stuart persisted, looking not at Sheena but turning her head a little to address someone who was standing in the further corner of the room and who now came forward.

Sheena glanced upwards and felt herself stiffen. It was the man to whom she had spoken in the inn; the man who had insulted Scotland by his cynical and rude remarks; the man she had hated all the way from the coast to Paris and thought perhaps she would never see again.

She had forced herself, when he had gone, not to ask any of her escort who he was and not to speak of him. Now she regretted that she had no idea of his identity. If he was in attendance on Mary Stuart, he was an enemy and she must beware of him.

'You have not welcomed Mistress McCraggan to France,' the Duchesse said quietly to Mary Stuart, and to Sheena's surprise the young Queen flushed slightly at the rebuke.

'Forgive me, Madame,' she said to the Duchesse, and turning to Sheena held out her hand. 'I do welcome you, I do truly,' she said. 'It must have been a long and tiring journey and it was very gracious of you to come to me.'

Sheena felt the young Queen's hands touch hers and in that moment she knew the full and fatal fascination of the Stuarts which could so cleverly and so skilfully charm all with whom they came into contact and make them in an instant their abject and adoring slaves.

She found herself holding on to the Queen's hand and stammering the words she had intended to speak and which had been in her mind when she first left Scotland.

'I have . . . come, Ma'am, to . . . to bring you the greetings, the love and . . . the devotion of all those who look on you as their . . . rightful Queen and to tell you that they are holding your kingdom for you if it means that . . . that every man in Scotland must die to do so.'

She spoke passionately, forgetting for a moment everything around her and seeing only the bare heads of the clansmen, the wind and rain in their faces, as her ship drew away from the quay.

'Thank you! Thank you!' Mary Stuart said. 'Tell them that my heart is with them.'

It was beautifully said and as Sheena felt the tears gather in her eyes, the voice of the man she so disliked intruded upon them.

'Well done,' she heard him say, and it seemed to Sheena that he broke the poignant spell between herself and Mary Stuart.

'I have not introduced you,' the Duchesse said. 'Mistress McCraggan, this is the Duc de Salvoire. Your Queen will tell you that there is no one in the whole of France who is cleverer at assessing the worth and performance of a horse. In fact none of us buy our horseflesh without his advice. Is that not so?'

The Duc bowed as Sheena dropped him a curtsy.

'You flatter me, Madame,' he said to the Duchesse. 'And somehow I do not think our visitor is interested in horses. Surely in Scotland they have eagles to carry them from place to place?'

He was mocking her and Sheena attempted to annihilate him with a glance and failed. Mary Stuart laughed.

'How ridiculous you are, your Grace!' she exclaimed. 'You make a joke of everything. But what a glorious idea. If we could be carried about by eagles, think how swiftly we could travel. Even swifter than your chestnuts can convey us—and that is saying a great deal.'

'Do not speak of his chestnuts,' the Duchesse appealed. 'The King is wild with envy and you know that he longs to buy them from you. Can I not plead with you once again to sell them to him?'

The Duc shook his head.

'What money could compensate me for the loss of such perfect animals?' he enquired. 'They should not be the objects of sale and barter. But, Madame, may I not present them to you as a tribute to your beauty and because, above all things, I enjoy your mind?'

'No, no, it is impossible,' the Duchesse said, and then with a sudden smile: 'I really believe you mean it. I warn you, if you make the offer again I shall accept, if only to make the King happy.'

The Duc made a little gesture with his hands.

'They are yours,' he said.

Sheena looked at them both with contempt. So he was toadying now to the King's mistress, this man she hated and despised; this man who she felt should have no contact with the child Queen she had come to protect and help.

Eagles indeed! He had laughed at her and made her feel a fool. Now he was making an extravagant gesture which would ingratiate him with the King who would be, whether he liked it or not, in his debt.

'Are you not lucky?' Mary Stuart was saying enviously. 'Oh, Madame, I wish the Duc had given the horses to me.'

'You shall share them with me,' the Duchesse said generously. 'When you want to use them on any special occasion, come and ask me. I will see that they are put at your disposal.'

'Oh, thank you,' Mary Stuart said. She put her arms round the Duchesse and gave her a hug.

Sheena could not help but shudder at the thought of such beauty and innocence embracing a woman who was old and steeped in sin.

'And now will you show Mistress McCraggan—you will not mind if I call you Sheena, will you, dear?—to her rooms?' the Duchesse said. 'They are on your corridor and I am sure that you girls will have a lot to talk about.'

'Come, let me show them to you,' Mary Stuart said, holding out her hand to Sheena.

At the touch of her fingers Sheena felt that her cup should be full of happiness. She was in France, hand in hand with the Queen. They were going away together, leaving behind them for a moment, at least, the wicked courtesan who had seduced the King, and the Duc, who she knew without the shadow of doubt was a bad and evil influence.

How much there was for her to do for the Queen! And yet, as they moved towards the door, she was conscious that it was Mary Stuart who led her. She was slower, less sophisticated, less assured, than this elegant, beautiful girl who was talking to her with an easy charm that was in itself irresistible.

'Your rooms are delightful,' she was saying. 'The Duchesse de Valentinois allowed me to choose the furniture for them myself. I will show you. . . .'

They had reached the door and were just about to pass through and as they did so Sheena heard the Duc say something to the Duchesse. He spoke in a low voice, but she caught the words quite clearly.

'You had better get the child some clothes, she needs them!'

3

The Duc de Salvoire climbed the twisting stairs which led from one part of the Palace to another. The candles had burned low in the sconces and where one had flickered out he banged his knee against a protruding pillar in the darkness and swore beneath his breath.

'I am getting too old at twenty-six for creeping along passages in the middle of the night,' he told himself wryly, with a twist of his lips which his enemies would have recognised as being an expression of his most caustic mood.

As he reached the wing which led to the Queen's apartments and those of her suite, he hesitated and for a moment considered returning the way he had come. And then with a shrug of his shoulders he realised that René would be waiting for him. It would be churlish and discourteous to cancel his appointment when he had not seen her alone for nearly three weeks and had been away at Anet for part of the time.

There were only two more passages, mercifully empty at this hour of the night, although he could hear the footsteps of a sentry in the distance. And then he was knocking on her door, two long knocks and a short, staccato one, before it was opened swiftly by a maidservant who kept her head down and did not raise her eyes from his feet from the moment when she dropped him a curtsy.

The Duc walked past her without a word and then was in the small, fragrantly scented boudoir which stood adjacent to a larger and more impressive bedchamber.

The Comtesse René de Pouguet was waiting for him. As

he entered the room and closed the door behind him, she rose from her chaise-longue on which she had been resting and came towards him eagerly.

She was strikingly attractive, with raven hair, slanting green eyes that gave her a seductive, mysterious expression which, however, was belied by her lips; about them there was no mystery, only the hunger and yearning of a passionate woman.

'Jarnac!' she exclaimed. 'I have been waiting so long. I thought perhaps you had forgotten me.'

'How could I do that?' the Duc enquired, bending his head to kiss the long, white fingers of her left hand on which glittered an enormous emerald ring.

As she moved with a serpentine grace, her robe of satin trimmed with ribbons and lace revealed that underneath it she wore very little, and there were tantalising glimpses of softly rounded breasts and beautifully shaped legs.

She used a heady, exotic perfume which seemed to permeate the whole room and mingle with the fragrance of lilies and tuberoses. There was also the hint of some other scent, something Oriental and incalculable, which made the Duc feel as if his senses were swimming a little.

Only a few tapers were lit and most of the light came from the half-open door of the bedchamber.

'You have missed me?'

It was a conventional question and now, with her lips parted, she looked up at him, her dark eyes glinting behind the incredibly long, black lashes.

'I was about to ask you that question.'

'Why did you spend so long with the Duchesse de Valentinois this evening?'

The Duc straightened his shoulders and there was a sudden guarded expression on his face.

'*Ma foi, René!*' he exclaimed. 'Is anything hidden from you? Have you an ear at every keyhole in the Palace?'

The Comtesse threw back her head and laughed.

'But, of course, *mon brave*! Do you not know that that

is why I am so useful and indispensable. If I were not the latter, do you know what my fate would be? To be sitting with my husband in the country looking at the crops and my only outing a drive to church on Sunday with my children grouped around me. It is a pretty picture but not one to my liking.'

The Duc knew that she spoke the truth. The Comte de Pouguet had retired from the Court a year ago, ostensibly to see to his estates in the Chambord district, but in reality because he could no longer afford his wife's extravagances or continually to turn a blind eye to her excesses.

The Comtesse had had countless protectors after his departure, but none had been so important, so wealthy or, indeed, so charming as the Duc de Salvoire.

Unfortunately, however, for René's peace of mind she had fallen in love. For the first time in her whole life her heart took precedence over her head. She loved the strange, cynical young man who she now suspected had taken her as his mistress merely because several of his friends had been competing for the honour and it had amused him to win far too easily what they coveted.

René might be shallow, but she was certainly not stupid. She was a lady-in-waiting to the Queen and had contrived to make herself so useful that if Catherine knew of her indiscretions she turned a blind eye to them.

René's love for the Duc, however, made her not so subtle in dealing with him as she would have been if her emotions had not been involved.

'You have not answered my question,' she insisted. 'Why were you so long with the "divine Diane"? Is is perhaps that you, too, find her divine?'

'We seem to have had this argument before,' the Duc said, surprisingly good-humouredly. 'I admire *Madame La Duchesse* enormously, as you well know, but I do not yet contemplate suicide by rivalling His Majesty for her attention.'

René laughed again.

'I am being stupid, I know that, but I am jealous—

jealous of all the time you spend away from me. I cannot think why you cannot take me to your estates in the country. Who would know if we went there by different roads? Oh, Jarnac, let us be alone together for a little while.'

She pressed herself close against him and laid her head on his shoulder. He put his arms around her, but almost perfunctorily, as if his mind was elsewhere.

'You have been with the Duchesse at Anet all the week,' she pouted, 'and yet when you come back to Paris you spend the evening with her while I wait alone and think that you will never come to me. Are you surprised that I feel hurt and a little resentful?'

'There is no need for either,' the Duc replied. 'The Duchesse had asked me to be present when she received Mistress Sheena McCraggan, the Scots girl who has arrived to take the place of Madame de Paroy, to whom Mary Stuart had taken an unreasoning and violent dislike.'

The Comtesse drew herself out of his arms.

'So the new *gouvernante* has arrived!' she exclaimed. 'I thought she was not due until tomorrow. What is she like? Is she pretty?'

'Small, attractive—yes, I think you would say distinctly pretty,' the Duc said.

'The Queen will be pleased,' the Comtesse murmured.

'The Queen! Why should she be interested?'

The question was sharp.

'Have you forgotten Lady Fleming?' the Comtesse enquired with a little sidelong glance of her eyes.

The Duc looked puzzled for a moment.

'Lady Fleming!' he repeated. 'Oh, you mean the previous governess who attracted the King for those few months when the Duchesse was ill and away from the Court.'

'So you do remember,' René smiled.

'A nasty scandal and one that should never have happened to anyone connected with Mary Stuart,' the Duc said almost harshly. Then added slowly: 'Do you mean that the Queen was pleased about that?'

René shrugged her almost naked shoulders.

'*Pourquoi pas?* The King's attention was diverted from the hated Diane. Even her witchcraft did not work when she was indisposed.'

'By all that is holy!' the Duc exclaimed. 'I have never heard such a monstrous idea, that the Queen should be pleased at her husband's indiscretion with a strange woman simply because it made him unfaithful to the woman he has adored since he was a young boy.'

'And who is eighteen years older than he!' the Comtesse said sharply. 'If that is not witchcraft I should like to know what is.'

'I will not discuss it,' the Duc retorted angrily. 'It is the Duchesse de Valentinois who has taught the King how to rule. Without her France would be in a sorry state today. If he loves her to the exclusion of all else, it is not surprising. But if the Queen or anyone else imagines that his devotion is likely to be forgotten or diverted by any little foreigner who comes tripping into the Palace on one pretext or another, they are very much mistaken.'

'How fortunate the Duchesse is to have such a champion,' René said softly, with a little edge on her voice which told all too clearly that she was piqued and annoyed by the turn the conversation had taken.

'What you have just suggested is disgusting and indecent,' the Duc said.

He walked across the room away from the Comtesse and then turned to look back at her. Her robe had slipped from one white shoulder and a long, slim thigh was revealed by the swift movement of her body.

She was enticing and seductive and they both knew it. And yet it seemed to him that for a moment the vision of another small face, with angry, flashing blue eyes and a trembling mouth, came between him and the woman seated at the end of the chaise-longue. It was a face haloed by unruly golden curls; a face with skin so white, so un-

36

blemished, that it seemed almost transparent.

He had not noticed until now, he thought suddenly, that René's skin was not her strongest point. It was slightly pock-marked, and though she was barely twenty-four there were already tiny lines at the corners of her eyes which were the toll of late nights and too much of the heady wine which she quaffed in golden goblets at the banquets given nightly at the Palace.

For a moment he felt almost repulsed by the thought of his lips on her red, expectant mouth. Then somehow the heat and the perfume of the room made him feel that any effort to escape from the inevitable was hardly worth while.

And so he stood looking at her as she rose very slowly to her feet; she swept back the rustling robe from her shimmering body and moved swiftly towards him. He felt her arms go round his neck and draw his head down to hers, felt her lips searching for his, and heard her whisper:

'Why are we talking? It is such a waste of time. Oh, Jarnac! Jarnac! I have missed you so much . . .'

In another part of the Palace, Sheena, too tired to sleep, tossed from side to side on the most comfortable bed she had ever known. There was so much to think about, so much to consider. And yet she was conscious that her overriding emotion was one of fear.

She had expected to feel small, insignificant and apprehensive in any Royal Palace. She had even expected that she would feel afraid in the presence of the King and the Queen. But what she had not anticipated was this feeling of being an utter failure, of having to return to those who had sent her and tell them there was nothing she could do, nothing she could say, because everything was completely and absolutely different from what they had imagined.

She had thought to find Mary Stuart a child. She found her a woman—and, what was more, a very educated young woman.

'It is really time that I should finish with lessons,' Mary

37

Stuart had said. 'I am proficient now in Latin, Greek, Spanish and Italian. When I insisted that Madame de Paroy should be dismissed, I had not thought that they would send me anyone else from Scotland.'

'I do not think that your statesmen meant to impose another teacher upon you,' Sheena said humbly. 'They sent me more as a . . . a companion.'

'I have many of those,' Mary Stuart said a little wearily, and then with that engaging, easy Stuart charm she added: 'But it is nice to have you here. A new face is always a *divertissement*. Come, you must meet the others.'

'No, no,' Sheena protested hastily. 'Not at this moment, please, Ma'am. Let us be alone together for a little while. There is so much I want to talk to you about, so much I have to tell you.'

'About Scotland?' Mary Stuart queried, and it seemed to Sheena there was a note of boredom in her voice. 'The others said you would come full of long speeches and addresses. The letters of the Elders are enough, I assure you. Sometimes they take nearly an hour to read and they write all the time about things of which I know nothing—the Reformers; the dissension among the clans; their solemn conclaves and dreary discussions! Oh, it is so boring. Let us forget about it. There are lots of interesting things to do. Can you play Pall Mall? It is a game we all enjoy.'

Sheena felt her heart sink. What could she tell her father, waiting anxiously for her report on the attitude of Mary Stuart towards the dissensious Scotland? How could she ever explain to this laughing, happy girl the horror and the privation her subjects were suffering not only from the persecution of the English but also from the poverty which stalked the land, taking more toll of helpless children and weakened women than were ever killed in battle?

'I expect you can ride,' Mary Stuart was chattering on. 'We must persuade the King to lend you one of his horses. The stables at the Château des Tournes are filled with the most magnificent horseflesh you have ever seen.'

Sheena murmured something.

'His Majesty says that I ride as well as I dance,' the young Queen boasted. 'I saw the Queen flush with anger when he said it. She is so jealous. She cannot bear him to pay anyone a compliment.'

'Perhaps Her Majesty has reason for her jealousy,' Sheena suggested quietly.

'Oh, nobody bothers about her!' Mary Stuart exclaimed. 'She is *très ennuyeuse* and when she sends for me I always try to make an excuse not to visit her. It is not always easy because *Madame La Duchesse* insists that I behave with the utmost courtesy to Her Majesty.'

'The Duchesse de Valentinois is right . . .' Sheena began, and then realised that she was siding with the woman whom she thought of as a natural enemy.

This moment of bewilderment was repeated again and again before she had left Mary Stuart to find her bedchamber and Maggie unpacking for her.

'Have ye seen Her wee Majesty?' Maggie enquired eagerly as she entered the room.

Sheena nodded.

'I have, indeed,' she answered. 'She is very lovely, Maggie, but she is no longer a child. We are not needed here.'

'Ah, now, Mistress Sheena, dinna ye go making up your mind about something like that within the first moment of your crossing the threshold. 'Tis not like'y that our Queen, after being in exile all these years, will not have learned to hide her true feelings and not to go about wearing her heart upon her sleeve. How is she to know at the first sight o' ye whether ye be friend or foe? And the Lord knows there's enough o' both in Scotland!'

'At least she knows I have come as a friend,' Sheena said.

'There's friends and friends!' Maggie muttered darkly. 'Dinna forget there are those in Scotland who have fought all the time against her mother, poor blessed lady. Do ye no' suppose that she is aware that they will be ready to fight against her when the time comes?'

'Yes, you are right!' Sheena exclaimed in tones of relief. 'Perhaps things will seem simpler and plainer tomorrow. At the moment I am in such a daze that I do not know what I do think.'

'Of course ye dinna,' Maggie answered stoutly.

It was then that without any warning Sheena found the tears running down her cheeks. It had been a long voyage. it had been unnerving to arrive at Brest to find there was no one there to meet her. Her encounter with the Duc, the elegance of her escort and the knowledge of her own insignificance and badly dressed appearance had all culminated in the shock of finding the little Queen she had come to instruct was not a helpless, homesick child.

She had thought to find Her Majesty lost and bewildered in the corrupt Court, instead she had discovered a poised and elegant young woman seemingly far older than herself, well educated, exquisitely mannered and already more *au fait* with the world and its affairs than Sheena could ever hope to be.

This was all too much to be borne, and hiding her face on Maggie's broad shoulder she sobbed:

'Let us go home. We are not wanted here, Maggie. Let us go home.'

'Now dinna fach yeself,' Maggie said soothingly.

She held Sheena close and then, when the tempest of her tears abated a little, fetched her a drink of water and with it a draught of what Maggie called her 'soothing medicine'.

She had no sooner drunk it than she began to feel unconscionably sleepy. She tried to protest, but Maggie took her clothes from her and helped her into bed.

'I must dress and go down to dinner,' she murmured. 'They will be expecting me.'

'There's plenty of time for that on the morrow,' Maggie said quietly.

The sheets smelt of lavender and were warm from the warming pan. Her tired body sank low in the goose-feather mattress.

'I will get up in five minutes,' she tried to say to Maggie,

40

but before the words were past her lips she was asleep.

Maggie found a chambermaid and told her to carry a message to the young Queen that Sheena was indisposed after the long journey and would not be able to come down to dinner that night. The chambermaid promised to deliver it to a footman, and Maggie, having seen that Sheena was asleep, drew the curtains quietly and went to her own room.

Sheena woke with a start feeling that something was wrong. The room was in darkness, the fire had burned low and she guessed that it must be in the early hours of the morning. She felt conscience-stricken that she should have failed in her new position so soon and so quickly after her arrival, but it was too late now to do anything about it and she knew that the wisest thing she could do would be to go back to sleep.

But this was the one thing which seemed impossible. Instead she began to toss and turn. Scraps of conversation came back to her—the expression on Mary Stuart's face when she had spoken of Scotland; the tone of contempt that it seemed to her had been in the Duc's voice as he told the Duchesse de Valentinois to get her some clothes.

'I should never have come,' she said forlornly to the darkness, and felt her heart ache because of the blindness of those scores of devoted men in Scotland, plotting and planning and worrying over their young Queen, quite unaware that she was a very different being from the baby they had seen carried aboard the ship which had taken her from them to the safety of France.

'How can I ever tell them? How can I make them understand?' Sheena asked.

She must have dozed a little. When she opened her eyes again, the light was coming through the curtains. It was the pale, faint, golden light of dawn; and because she felt stifled by the comfort of her feather bed and over-soft pillows, she rose and crossed the room to throw wide the long windows which reached the floor.

She found herself looking out over the courtyard beyond which were the gardens of the Palace. There was the sound of horses' hoofs below and Sheena craned her head forward. A magnificent white stallion was being led into the courtyard. The embroidered reins and velvet-covered saddle made her guess that it belonged to someone of importance.

Did the King rise at such an early hour? she wondered, and guessed by the light on the horizon that it was not yet six o'clock. Then down the steps below her she saw a figure she recognised.

It was the Duchesse de Valentinois. She heard her voice, low, musical, wishing the grooms good morning and saying a word of greeting to the horse itself. Then she sprang into the saddle with the elasticity and grace of a young girl, her foot barely resting in the cupped hand of the page who knelt to assist her.

With only a groom in attendance the Duchesse cantered away over the cobblestones, her lovely face raised towards the sun as if she would drink in the beauty and freshness of it.

Sheena stared after her in astonishment. How could the Duchesse be up so early when she was so old and when she must have been late last night at dinner with the King? It was yet another of the puzzling things which she was finding in this strange Palace in this strange land.

Somehow she had had in her mind a picture of how wicked people behaved—drinking, making love and gambling all night and staying in bed half the day because they were too tired to rise as ordinary people had to do. This was certainly not true of the Duchesse de Valentinois.

Sheena felt that she could not sleep again and so she dressed herself, knowing it was far too early to leave her room. She settled herself at the small escritoire in the corner and tried to begin a letter to her father.

'I will write the moment I arrive,' she had promised him. Yet what was there to say except to tell him how bad the voyage had been, how Maggie had succumbed to the waves and how there had been no one there to meet her when she had arrived at the quayside?

She put all this down on paper and then stopped. How could she go on? Was she to tell him about the Duc and how she disliked him? Was she to recount her first impressions of Madame de Valentinois? Could she possibly describe in words the look on the King's face when the Duchesse had come into the room and it seemed as if he was suddenly lit by a light from within to become, before her very eyes, a different man altogether?

And Mary Stuart, Queen of Scotland! What could she write of her?

There was the sound of more horses' hoofs outside, and Sheena, glad of the excuse, rose and went to the window. She looked down into the courtyard expecting to see the Duchesse returning, but now she saw that it was the King who was mounting a splendid black horse and that there were four of his gentlemen to squire him.

'Which way did *Madame La Duchesse* go?' she heard him ask one of the grooms.

The man pointed out the direction and the King rode off eagerly. Another person rising early and contradicting all her assumptions as to what was likely to happen in this great, luxurious Palace.

Sheena went back to her desk, but she had not been there long before there was a discreet knock at the door. She opened it, wondering if it was Maggie who had come to her, but found instead a page with a note on a silver salver.

She opened it and looking quickly at the signature saw that it read: *Gustave de Cloude*, and remembered that he was one of the young men who had escorted her from Brest to Paris.

I have seen you at your window, he wrote, *so I know you are awake. Will you not meet me in the garden? There are many things I should like to speak to you about while the rest of the Palace is asleep.*

Sheena hesitated. She felt it would be indiscreet and perhaps something which would be frowned on, that she should walk in the gardens with a man she knew so slightly. And yet at the same time she was curious. She longed to ask questions of someone, anyone, who could answer what she wanted to know.

The small page stood there solemnly looking at her.

'Are you waiting for an answer?' she asked him.

'I am waiting, Ma'mse'le, to escort you to the garden,' he replied, with a little bow which made her smile because it was such a perfect imitation of his master's.

She suddenly felt young and gay and the troubles and anxieties of the night fell away from her.

'I will come for a few minutes,' she said, more to herself than to him, and picking up her shawl she slipped it over her shoulders. 'Show me where the Comte is waiting.'

'I will take you to him immediately, Ma'mselle,' the page promised.

They went down a twisting maze of corridors and staircases which made Sheena think that she would never find her way to the ground floor, when suddenly they emerged not into the courtyard but into the garden itself by a side entrance which led directly on to the terrace and formal lawns where a fountain was playing.

There was no sign of anyone until the page led her down a twisting, lavender-hedged path and through two cypress trees standing sentinel over a herb garden which was hidden from the windows of the Palace.

It was then that she saw the Comte sitting on a marble seat by a small goldfish pool, the early sun shining on his polished dark head.

He sprang up eagerly at her approach and came towards her, then taking her hand in his he raised it to his lips.

'I hardly dared to hope that you would come,' he said in a low voice.

Sheena smiled at him.

'It was kind of you to ask me,' she said. 'I was feeling lost and I think a little homesick. I wanted so much to talk to someone.'

'And I wanted to talk to you,' he replied. 'It was impossible while I was your escort with three of my friends listening to everything that we might have said. But now it is different. You are so lovely! I have been able to think of nothing else since I first met you.'

The tone in his voice made Sheena feel embarrassed. She dropped her eyes, conscious that he was still holding her hand.

'Enchanting and an enchantress,' he smiled. 'Come and sit down and let me look at you.'

'Please, you must not pay me compliments,' Sheena said.

'Why not?' he asked in genuine astonishment.

'I am not used to them,' she answered. 'In Scotland no gentleman would think of saying such things on so short an aquaintance. And, besides, I have come into the garden because I want to talk to you on serious matters.'

The Comte laughed.

'How can we be serious?' he asked. 'And, indeed, why should we be? We are young and alone and I am very much in love.'

'Please . . . please . . .' Sheena murmured, feeling with something like panic that she should not have left her room.

She made a little movement, but now the Comte had both her hands in his and was covering them with kisses.

'You are adorable,' he said softly. 'How can I talk to you when all I want to do is to tell you that you have set me on fire. I can think only of your hands, your eyes, your lips. . . .'

He bent towards her as he spoke and now, really frightened and realising how stupid she had been to accept his invitation, Sheena exerted all her strength and managed to free her hands from his. Then, lifting her skirts, she ran hastily back the way she had come, leaving him calling after her, her woollen shawl lying at his feet.

She ran helter-skelter down the garden, between the cypress trees and across the terrace towards the door into the Palace through which the page had led her. She found it and pulled it open, only to be confronted by a choice of several passages.

Wildly, half afraid that the Comte would follow her, she turned left, only to realise after she had been running for a few seconds that she had chosen wrongly. The passage broadened into a wide hall. She saw an open doorway which she realised led into the courtyard and knew she must retrace her steps.

She halted, but it was too late. Someone coming into the hall from the other direction saw her and crossed the polished floor to her side. She tried to turn back but he put a hand on her arm and prevented her.

'Mistress McGraggan! What are you doing here?' he asked.

She looked up at the Duc de Salvoire and saw his face, dark and unsmiling, and with a little stab of horror realised how she must look to him, her hair dishevelled, her cheeks flushed from running, her hands trembling.

'It is . . . it is a m . . . mistake,' she stammered. 'Please let me go. I . . . I didn't mean to come this way.'

'Let me show you the right staircase,' he said quietly.

She was too frightened to argue with him and too lost to protest her independence. With her breath coming unevenly in quick gasps she was forced to move beside him down the passage, one hand creeping up to try to subdue the curls over her forehead.

'What has frightened you?' he asked gently.

'N . . . nothing, your Grace. It was . . . just that I . . . I lost my way.'

She felt her cheeks burn furiously now at the lie, and yet, she asked herself, what else could she say? If only he would not find out how stupid she had been.

'It is very easy to do that in this Palace,' he said in his quiet, bored voice. 'And that is why it is wisest, until you become more accustomed to the many entrances and exits, to take your maid with you or to go accompanied by one of the ladies-in-waiting of Mary Stuart. You will meet them this morning. I hope you will find some congenial friends amongst them.'

'I think that is unlikely,' Sheena said, surprised into speaking the truth. Her voice was low and miserable and the moment she had spoken the words she regretted them.

The Duc stopped walking and looked down at her.

'I thought the Scots were fighters,' he said. 'I thought they had, if nothing else, more courage than anyone else.'

Sheena felt herself quiver at his words. They flicked her on the raw. At the same time, in all honesty, she had to admit they were justified. Because she had no one else to ask she had to ask of him the question that had been torturing her all night.

'You do not think,' she said in a voice little above a whisper, 'that it would be best if I returned home now, at once?'

Because she hated him and she knew his supreme indifference to herself, she felt his answer would be honest— perhaps more honest than anyone else's would have been.

'No! ' he said unexpectedly abruptly. 'Put your chin up and face it. Do what you have come to do.'

Instinctively they had stopped walking and now their eyes met. For a moment she gazed at him, knowing that he had said what she ought to hear and yet somehow dismayed because he had said it. And then, even as he had commanded her, her chin went up.

'Thank you,' she said, almost beneath her breath. 'You have answered my question for me. I will try not to be afraid.'

'There is nothing to be afraid of, really,' he said. 'You will find that most of our fears are inside ourselves, not outside.'

Sheena glanced at him quickly and then almost as if he was sorry he had said so much he pointed ahead to where there was a staircase just a little to the right of the door from which he had entered the garden.

'That is the way you should have taken,' he said abruptly and uncompromisingly.

She opened her lips to thank him and then as she did so, through the open door which led to the garden, she saw coming across the terrace straight towards them the Comte de Cloude. He was looking annoyed and he was carrying in his hand a woollen shawl which seemed to Sheena to shriek in every homemade stitch of it that it came from Scotland.

She saw the Duc glance towards the Comte; she saw his lips tighten and knew he understood what had happened. She thought she saw an expression of contempt in his eyes, the same contempt that she had suspicioned had been there at other times.

And then, because the situation was beyond her, because she felt that anything she did or said would make matters worse, without another word she ran forward and up the stairs which the Duc had indicated to her.

She ran so quickly that by the time she reached the top her heart was pounding and it was hard to breathe. In fact she might have had two devils instead of one at her heels!

4

'What must he think of me? What must he think of me?'

Sheena felt the words pounding against her brain as she ran headlong up the stairs, the colour in her cheeks due not only to the exertion of climbing so quickly but also to humiliation.

Why had he looked at her like that? Why had the Duc's bored, steel-grey eyes seemed to hold a reproach? Or was she mistaken and it was only condemnation and disgust?

How could she have known for one moment that the Comte was going to behave in such a manner? Sheena, in all innocence, thought that love was something which was kept for the evening or the night. Whispered words in the moonlight, or perhaps the quick pressure of a hand as a woman danced with a man who attracted her or ran as dusk fell to meet him at some secret assignation.

This was morning, in the sunlight. And then she remembered that it was also France. Little wonder that her father and the Elders of Scotland had spoken in shocked voices of French morals and had felt that Mary Stuart might be contaminated by the looseness of French ways.

Sheena reached the top of the narrow staircase and had to stop a moment to get her breath. She was on a landing which she vaguely recognised and then as she stood there, her small breasts heaving tumultuously, she heard a shriek of laughter, heard a door open and saw one of the chambermaids come running into the passage followed by one of the flunkeys. She tried to elude him, but he caught her amid what were quite obviously ineffectual protests and she allowed herself to be soundly kissed before they disappeared once again into the doorway through which they had come.

'Like master, like maid,' The old adage came to Sheena's mind and her lip curled. This was France and she must be on her guard, not only for Mary Stuart but for herself.

Soberly she walked down the corridor, remembering now in which direction her apartment lay. She had learned her lesson, she told herself; and then unbidden the question came to her mind:

Would the Duc understand? Would he put her behaviour down to ignorance or merely to wantonness?

'It does not matter to me what he thinks,' she told herself defiantly. And yet she knew that because she hated him she did not wish to give him any excuse to disparage her.

Quite suddenly the enormity of her task which lay ahead struck her so forcibly that she paused once again to look out of the window on to the formal gardens. How could she, so ignorant, so badly equipped for a life like this, try to understand the machinations and intrigues of this great Palace?

With something suspiciously like a sob Sheena continued her journey towards her own bedchamber. She opened the door to find Maggie standing by the bed.

'Where have ye been, ye bad bairn?' she said in her scolding voice. ' 'Tis worried stiff I've been about ye. No one seemed to know where ye'd gone.'

'It is all right, Maggie,' Sheena said a little wearily. 'I have come to no harm. I merely went for a walk in the garden.'

'At such an hour! And the little Queen herself asking for ye.'

'Mary Stuart asking for me?' Sheena said quickly, the life coming back to her face.

'Yes, indeed! Her Majesty wishes you to go with her to watch the King play tennis, and after that . . .'

Before Maggie could say more Sheena interrupted her with a little cry.

'What is this? Where did it come from?' she asked, for she had seen lying on the bed a magnificent and very beautiful gown of white satin embroidered with blue jewels and tiny pearls caught with blue ribbons over a petticoat of exquisite lace.

It was so beautiful as to leave Sheena gasping at it in astonishment and admiration.

'Ye may well ask,' Maggie said triumphantly. ' 'Tis a present for ye.'

'A present!' Sheena's voice sharpened. 'I will not accept it.'

All too clearly she could hear the Duc's scornful, drawling voice as he said to the Duchesse de Valentinois: 'You had better get the child some clothes. She needs them.'

Stamping her foot Sheena turned away from the gown and walked across the room as if to get away from it as far as possible.

'I will not accept it,' she said again. 'Take it back.'

'Take it back?' Maggie echoed in a bewildered voice. 'But for why?'

'Because I say so,' Sheena snapped. 'I will wear my

own clothes—clothes that were good enough for Scotland but are not good enough for me here! Well, I will not be the first to complain.'

'But, Mistress Sheena, 'tis crazy!' Maggie expostulated. 'When they asked last night for your measurements I was that happy, for I knew even before we left home that your clothes were not right. Och, I'm not saying that your father didna fork from his pocket as much as he could afford, or that Mistress Macleod didna sew to the very best o' her ability. But one look at the ladies that ye see here must ha' told ye that ye look a rare scarecrow with your narrow skirts and thick woollen shawls.'

'Nevertheless, that is what I shall wear,' Sheena said sharply. 'Take the gown back and tell *Madame La Duchesse* that I do not accept gifts from strangers.'

'*Madame La Duchesse!*' Maggie exclaimed. 'But 'tis not she who has sent ye this gown.'

'Not the Duchesse!' Sheena repeated the words in astonishment. 'Well, who then?'

'The Queen herself!' Maggie replied. 'Nay, not Her wee Majesty—from all accounts she finds it hard to scrape enough money together for her own gowns. Nay, 'tis Queen Catherine who has sent ye this magnificent gown—and with a promise of more to come.'

'Queen Catherine!'

Sheena could hardly say the words aloud, she was so surprised. She had not expected that the Queen would have even heard of her arrival, let alone be considerate for her well-being.

Impulsively she rushed across the room to the bed, fingering the gown and holding it up against her, then seeking a mirror in which she could see her reflection.

'But how kind! How very, very kind of Her Majesty,' she said. 'How could she know I needed such gowns and I have not even met her yet?'

'They say the Queen has her ways of knowing everything that goes on in the Palace,' Maggie said, 'for all that she's so meek and quiet and appears to mind nothing—

not even being forgotten and ignored at times.'

'She must mind that,' Sheena said.

'Nay, for she makes a great fuss of *Madame La Duchesse* in public and when she is in childbirth they say 'tis the Duchesse herself who ministers to her and even brings the wee bairn into the world.'

Sheena turned round.

'Maggie, how do you know all this?'

'Know it!' Maggie snorted. ' 'Tis very little I dinna know by this time. Never have I heard such a lot of gossips as there be below stairs.'

'But how can you understand them?' Sheena asked. 'You have never learned the language.'

'Och, that's no barrier in this place,' Maggie replied. 'Why, there are plenty o' Scots to be found and ye can be sure they made a beeline for me when I arrived to hear the latest news from home.'

Sheena looked incredulous and Maggie went on:

' 'Twere the maids who came with Her wee Majesty and who stayed here ever since, and there are several valets who crossed the sea with visitors from the North, then found it convenient not to return home. There's good money here, Mistress Sheena. Good money, good food and a deal more comfort than we are used to at home.'

'So you have found friends,' Sheena said quietly and with a note of envy in her voice.

'Aye, that I have,' Maggie answered. 'And talk! Ye'd think they wanted to tell me the whole history o' France in a single night.'

'You say the Queen accepts the Duchesse de Valentinois?'

'Indeed she does! But there are whispers that her meekness is but a mask and underneath she longs to destroy her and her power over the King.'

'It would be more human if she felt like that,' Sheena said.

Maggie shrugged her shoulders—a gesture which Sheena noticed with amusement, thinking it would be an already newly acquired trick that she had adopted from her Frenchified countrymen.

But she could not worry very much about Maggie. The gown which she held in her hands was so magnificent that it drew her eyes to the exclusion of all else.

'If the Queen has sent me this,' she said in tones of joy, 'I can accept it and gratefully.'

'It is, indeed, kind of Her Majesty,' Maggie said. 'What is more, she wishes to see ye.'

'She has asked for me too?' Sheena said.

'That she has,' Maggie replied. 'And when I told the maid that Her wee Majesty was waiting for ye, she said that Mary Stuart herself would take ye there after you had watched the King at tennis.'

Sheena forgot to be worried and anxious and let out a little whoop of joy.

'Then help me into this gown, Maggie,' she said. 'Never, never did I think to possess anything so magnificent or so beautiful. Pray Heaven it becomes me!'

She need not have worried. With her fair skin and red-go'd hair the white gown with its blue and pearl embroidery made her look so entrancing that she could hardly believe it was herself that she saw in the silver mirror.

Maggie tried to dress her hair a little formally, and although soft tendrils of curls would escape, the result when she had finished made Sheena feel regal as well as lovely.

She could not help the thought flashing through her mind that if the Comte had found her desirable this morning, what would he think of her now? She could still hear his impassioned voice and feel the imprint of his hot lips on her hand.

She had been afraid and flustered; but now she told herself that she had been ridiculous. Only a country bumpkin would have been unable to cope with such a situation. She should have rebuked him, told him to behave himself and talked seriously and quietly, which should have calmed his passion. A clever woman, she thought, would keep any man at arm's length, however ardent.

Then, with a little sinking of her heart, she told herself that she was not clever. She saw herself standing with crimson cheeks before the Duc; she saw herself running away as the Comte approached carrying her woollen shawl.

How gauche; how naive; how utterly humiliating! She should have stood her ground and held her head high. She should have shown the Duc that the blood that coursed through her veins could give her courage and control of her emotions.

Instinctively, as she watched herself in the mirror, her chin went up. This gown would give her courage. She would be cool and gracious and not in the least apologetic for what was not her fault.

'Ye look a real picture,' Maggie was saying. 'I wouldn'a have believed it possible. No one would recognise ye, not even your own father.'

'That is what I want,' Sheena said almost beneath her breath. 'I want them to forget the girl who arrived here yesterday.'

Maggie looked at her in surprise, but there was no time for explanations. There was a knock at the door and a flunkey reminded them that the Queen of Scotland was still awaiting her.

Sheena swept out into the passage and followed the footman to the apartments of Mary Stuart. She was very conscious as she moved of the rustle of silk around her feet, of the tight boning of her bodice, the smallness of her waist.

She caught a glimpse of herself in the long, gilt mirrors which were interspersed between the pictures in the corridors. She was well aware that a lady and gentleman passing her turned to look back, asking themselves, no doubt, who she was. It was a heady, exciting feeling to know that one was being admired, to feel of consequence for the first time in one's life.

They reached the little Queen's apartments and as Sheena swept in through the door Mary Stuart sprang from her escritoire where she was writing and exclaimed:

'You have come at last! I began to think you had not got my message.'

Sheena sank down in a deep curtsy.

'Forgive me, Your Majesty,' she said apologetically. 'I have been waiting to change.'

'*Mon Dieu*! What a gorgeous gown!' Mary Stuart said admiringly. She had been speaking English, but now, as if it were easier, she burst into French. ' 'Tis ravishing, enchanting! Where did you get anything so lovely? Surely there are not gowns like this in Scotland?'

'No, indeed,' Sheena said honestly. 'I have never seen anything so exquisite before. It has been given me by Queen Catherine.'

'Queen Catherine!' Mary Stuart exclaimed in surprise. 'Then it cannot be hers. She must have purloined it from one of her ladies-in-waiting: perhaps the little Comtesse de St. Vincente, who is reputed to have more gowns than anyone else in the whole of France. She is about your size.'

'However she came by it, it is indeed gracious of Her Majesty. How kind she must be, how thoughtful for others,' Sheena said, taking advantage of the opportunity to point out the Queen's virtues.

She saw an expression she did not understand on Mary Stuart's face. It seemed as if she were about to speak and then changed her mind, pressing her cupid's-bow mouth together as if in an effort to bite back the words.

'Come,' she said a little awkwardly. 'We must go to the tennis courts or His Majesty will wonder where we are.'

'Do you usually watch His Majesty play?' Sheena asked as they went down the broad staircase side by side.

'He likes an audience,' Mary Stuart answered. 'What man does not? They all want to be applauded and told how clever they are, while we are longing for their compliments and jealous of their preoccupation with themselves.'

The young Queen's words left Sheena with a sense of dismay. What would they think in Scotland of such sentiments? Why, indeed, should this child—for she was little more—know so much about men? Why, oh why, had she been brought to this Court at an early age and never had a chance to return home?

As if she sensed there was criticism, Mary Stuart pressed all her weapons of charm and endearment into the smile she gave Sheena.

'It is delightful to have you here,' she said. 'I have many friends, but it is fun to have one more. I was saying only this morning that we must teach you all the arts and graces of the Court. It is difficult for someone new not to commit gaucheries or to make mistakes.'

'I shall be very grateful if you can prevent my doing that, Ma'am,' Sheena said.

'We must try,' the Queen smiled, 'and I think, looking at you now in that lovely gown, there will be a great many people willing to teach you—especially those of the opposite sex.'

Sheena tried to remember that she had come to instruct the Queen, not vice versa; but it was impossible to do anything but follow Mary Stuart into the gay, laughing crowd who were seated or standing on the lawns around the tennis-court watching the King playing what Sheena realised was a strenuous and extremely skilful game with three of his courtiers.

She had never seen tennis before. At first Mary Stuart and then several gentlemen standing around tried to explain to her the intricacies of the game. What surprised her was the King's skill and the fact that, playing in his shirt-sleeves with his lace cuffs floating in the breeze, there was nothing to single him out as being a king or to distinguish him from the other players.

They had not been there more than a few minutes when the company parted as the Duchesse de Valentinois came moving over the lawns with an exquisite grace that was somehow peculiarly her own.

She was dressed in a white gown with touches of black—the colours, Mary Stuart whispered, that were her own and were also worn as a livery by all her servants.

'Why black and white?' Sheena asked.

56

'She vowed after her husband's death to mourn for him always,' the little Queen replied with an impish smile. 'But nobody will deny that such colours are particularly flattering to her hair and her skin.'

'They are, indeed,' Sheena said in grudging admiration.

'Three redheads!' Mary Stuart replied with a grin. 'The Duchesse, you and me! We ought to be able to get up to some mischief, ought we not?'

Sheena's first impulse was to reply lightly, and then she remembered her role as governess and said demurely:

'I think there are more important and serious things to do, Ma'am. I want, when you will permit me the time, to speak to you of Scotland,'

Mary Stuart's face did not change, nor did she say anything. But Sheena had the feeling that she had withdrawn from her even though they were still standing side by side. She had a feeling of hopelessness, of being confronted suddenly with a blank wall. And then the voice she hated said from behind her:

'And what does our visitor think of His Majesty's skill?'

He was mocking her, Sheena thought, knowing full well that she would never have seen tennis before and have no standard by which to compare the King with anyone else. Fortunately Mary Stuart had plenty to say.

'There are so many things I am going to show Mistress McCraggan,' she said. 'I cannot believe that amongst the snow and barren mountains of Scotland there are many amusements. We must entertain her, *Monsieur Le Duc*; show her that in France we can still be elegant and gay even when we are at war.'

'Which we are not at the moment,' the Duc replied.

'Oh, are we not?' Mary Stuart asked lightly. 'To be sure, I am never quite certain. One day we are marching over the Spanish border and the next day we are marching back. I was never very bloodthirsty for detail.'

'Your Majesty has no need to worry your head about anything so brutal as war!' the Duc said.

Sheena gave a little gasp.

'On the contrary, your Grace,' she interposed. 'Her Majesty's subjects are fighting at this very moment on her behalf—fighting valiantly and against almost overwhelming odds, to keep her kingdom intact.'

Sheena threw the words at him like a challenge and she had the satisfaction of seeing him, for the moment, look discomfited. And yet it was only for a moment.

'Your pardon, Ma'mselle,' he said. 'I was meaning that in the affairs of France Her Majesty need not concern herself. With superb diplomacy the King has managed to keep the peace since last January.'

It was not what he had meant, Sheena thought angrily. He had forgotten Scotland, just as Mary Stuart was in danger of forgetting it, and she clenched her fingers together in an effort not to be rude, not to tell him that there were better, finer and braver men in Scotland than were ever likely to be found fighting for France.

She bit back the words and at that moment the Duchesse de Valentinois joined them. Sheena curtsied, but stiffly and not very low.

'Did I hear you praising the King?' she said to the Duc, with the smile which made even her enemies feel as if the sun had come out.

'When I do so,' the Duc answered, 'it is obvious that I also pay homage to your Grace, for we all know how much we owe to your statesmanship, your magnificent handling of the political situation.'

'You are very kind, Monsieur,' the Duchesse said, but she did not contradict him. Instead she glanced across the tennis-court with an expression on her face which seemed to Sheena almost maternal. 'In two minutes I must interrupt him,' she said. 'Who would be a King? One cannot enjoy oneself for half an hour without the heavy cares of State volleying back at one far more forcibly than any opponent can strike.'

'The game is just finishing,' the Duc told her. 'Would you like me to fetch His Majesty?'

'Please,' the Duchesse said gently.

Sheena watched the Duc cross the court, saw that the King hardly waited for him to speak before he came quickly, with long strides, to where the Duchesse was waiting.

He raised her hand to his lips. It was no perfunctory gesture. His lips lingered for a moment on the softness of her skin and Sheena saw his fingers tighten on hers.

'You want me?'

'I am afraid so, Sire. The Ambassadors are here. We cannot begin without you.'

'No, no, of course not,' he said. 'Although you could have handled them far better than I.'

'I still need your authority, Sire.'

She smiled into his eyes and Sheena saw his face lighten as if some invisible message passed between them. Then he turned to thank those who had p'ayed with him and walked away with the Duchesse towards another entrance to the Palace.

'I told you we should be late,' Mary Stuart said in a disappointed tone. 'You have not even seen the King play a full game. Never mind! We must come tomorrow. Now we had best go and visit Her Majesty.'

She spoke reluctantly and Sheena forced an eager note into her voice as she said:

'It is most kind of you to take me. I am very anxious to meet Queen Catherine.'

Again she had the impression that Mary Stuart was withdrawing from her. Then before she could be sure of it the young Queen turned to the Duc and said:

'Mistress McCraggan has received a present from Her Majesty, and a very fine one at that. Do you not admire her appearance, Monsieur?'

'Naturally,' the Duc answered in his slow, slightly cynical voice. 'I was amazed at the transformation. But what has that to do with the Queen?'

'Everything,' Mary Stuart replied. 'The gown was a present.'

'From the Queen?'

59

The Duc's voice suddenly held a sharp note and Sheena realised that he glanced across the lawn to where the Duchesse and the King were disappearing through an opening in a clipped yew hedge.

'Yes, indeed,' Mary Stuart said. 'It is unlike Her Majesty to be so generous. I have received nothing from her save at festivals.'

'Her Majesty doubtless has her reasons,' the Duc said, and Sheena felt there was something else behind the words, something she could not understand, something which made her vaguely uncomfortable.

And then before she could reply there was a sudden cry, the sound of voices shouting from the direction in which the Duchesse and the King had gone. Instinctively and quickly everyone surged in the direction of the noise.

It took them only a few seconds to move across the lawns, to pass through the opening in the yew hedge and to find themselves outside one of the entrances to the Palace in the big, beautifully shaped courtyard at the end of which were wrought-iron gates opening on to the road.

Mary Stuart and Sheena seemed to be almost the first to reach the courtyard. They saw the Duchesse and the King standing on the steps leading to the Palace, while in front of them was a collection of men wearing the sombre garments of respectable tradesmen.

They appeared ordinary and harmless enough, but one of them, a man with flashing eyes and an unkempt beard, was shouting in a country dialect which made it difficult at first to understand what he said. Then with a kind of sick horror Sheena found herself translating the words.

'Harlot! Prostitute! You have sucked France dry and humbled all decency and respectability to the dust. You have seduced and corrupted the King. You have brought him down to the level of debauchery that is part of your trade.'

The man was still shouting as the guards came hurrying across the cobbled courtyard and seized him and his friends. None of the men made the slightest resistance, but

the one who had been speaking went on shouting: 'Wanton!|
Whore! Harlot!' until a blow in the mouth from one of
the guards dragging him along silenced his voice and
brought a rush of blood from between his lips.

Sheena felt paralysed with what was happening, as apparently was everybody else; she could only stare as the
men were dragged away, then she saw the King make a
hasty movement as if he would follow them.

The Duchesse put out her hand and laid it on his arm.
She was very pale but otherwise completely composed,
and still with her hand on the King's arm she went up the
steps and without a backward glance disappeared into the
Palace.

'Who are they? What does it mean?' Sheena asked almost beneath her breath, because there was something
horrible and almost indecent both in the words the man
had used and the hatred in his voice.

'I think they are Protestors,' Mary Stuart said. 'People
who are against the true faith.'

'Is that who they are?' Sheena said. 'We have them in
Scotland too.'

She was thinking of the tales that had been brought to
her father of how the little Queen's mother had been denounced in public by an unknown fanatic called John
Knox.

'How could they have got in here?' she heard one of
the gentlemen of the Court ask angrily.

'Perhaps they are encouraged,' the Duc answered.

'Encouraged!' the questioner ejaculated, but before
any more could be said the Duc walked away, following
the King and the Duchesse up the steps and into the Palace.

Sheena watched him go. The scene she had just wit-
nessed had been disturbing, terrifying and unpleasant. She
felt Mary Stuart take her hand in hers.

'Come,' she said. 'There is nothing we can do. It is best
to ignore these people. There are only a few of them and
the Duchesse will see that they are burned at the stake.'

'Burned at the stake!' Sheena repeated the words automatically. It was horrifying that a man should burn to death, whatever crime he had committed.

'Yes, indeed,' Mary Stuart said almost gleefully. 'The Duchesse insists on the death penalty for such rebels. It is said that the Holy Father has sent her his special blessing for the work she is doing in trying to stamp out heresy.'

'How could they be so mad to come here knowing what the penalty might be?' Sheena asked.

'Oh, they want to be martyrs, I suppose,' Mary Stuart replied. 'Do not let us think about them. It is too boring. This is not the first time it has happened and I expect the King will have something to say to the Captain of the Guard.'

'How, indeed, could the sentinels have let them through?' Sheena asked.

Mary Stuart gave her a little sideways glance.

'Did you not see what uniform the guards were wearing today?' she questioned.

'I do not think I noticed,' Sheena answered, 'and if I did it would convey little to me. I am afraid I am not yet conversant with the French regiments.'

'No, of course not,' Mary Stuart said. 'If you were it might seem significant to you. But never mind, let us see the Queen and get it over.'

There was so much impatience in her voice that somehow Sheena did not dare to argue further. Instead she followed the young Queen back through the garden and in through another entrance to the Palace. A sentry saluted them and she thought that they wore the same uniforms as the sentries in the courtyard, but she could not be sure.

They were met in the crystal and golden hall by a gentleman-at-arms, resplendent in gold and decorations, but with an expression of such cynicism on his face that Sheena had the uneasy impression that he thought his position was not good enough for him.

They climbed the stairs, waited for only a short while in the audience chamber and then a magnificent gentleman-at-arms said that Her Majesty was ready for them.

Sheena had expected someone small and oppressed with unhappy eyes and the uncertain manner of someone who is being persecuted. Instead, to her astonishment, she saw a fat dumpy little woman with an ugly face, protruding eyes and the quick, interested manner of someone who is alert and inquisitive.

The room was dark and rather badly decorated. The Queen, while covered with jewels and wearing a gown embroidered and enriched with satin and lace, somehow contrived to look dowdy.

She embraced Mary Stuart and turned to Sheena, who had sunk in a deep curtsy to the ground.

'Mistress Sheena McCraggan,' she said, speaking with a pronounced Italian accent. 'It is good to see you here. We are delighted you could come.'

Sheena rose and then the Queen exclaimed with delight:

'You are pretty and your hair is red! That is good, very good.'

Sheena was astonished at her words but hurried to express her thanks.

'It is indeed gracious of Your Majesty to send me this magnificent gown,' she said. 'I had not expected such kindness nor, indeed, such a generous gift. It is difficult for me to find words to express my pleasure and my gratitude.'

'There will be more. Yes, there will be more,' the Queen said. 'You are very small, so it was difficult to find you something to wear until the gowns I have ordered for you will be ready.'

'You have ordered gowns for me, Your Majesty!' Sheena exclaimed. 'It is an overwhelming gesture! Why should you be so kind?'

'You are grateful; that is all we want to hear,' the Queen replied, with a little pat on her shoulder.

Her hand was heavy with rings but Sheena could not help noticing that her fingernails were not very clean and she smelt slightly musty beneath the waves of heavy perfume with which she had enveloped herself.

'You are pretty, very pretty,' the Queen remarked with

satisfaction. 'A little later we must have a talk, just you and I together.'

'It will be a great honour, Your Majesty,' Sheena answered, feeling again that sense of bewilderment and astonishment.

'But now I have someone waiting for me,' the Queen told her.

She turned her head as she spoke, and one of her ladies-in-waiting, a plain gaunt woman, said quietly:

'He is here, Your Majesty.'

'Good! Good!' the Queen exclaimed delightedly. 'We must not keep him waiting. Goodbye, Mistress Mc-Craggan.'

She gave Sheena her hand and smiled on her little gold head as she swept down in a deep curtsy. Then she went from the room followed by her ladies-in-waiting and Mary Stuart and Sheena were left alone.

'Pouf! This place stinks!' Mary Stuart said in a whisper. 'Let us get out.'

They hurried almost guiltily down the stairs to the entrance. Sheena was trying to find words with which to praise the Queen for her kindness, but somehow it was difficult to know what to say.

'I'll wager that was the Queen's new necromancer whom she was so excited about,' Mary Stuart said as they reached the open air.

Sheena looked puzzled.

'Oh, did you not know?' Mary Stuart asked. 'That is all she is interested in—fortune-tellers, astrologers, crystal-gazers. She has dozens of them around her. I used to think it was rather fun to consult them, but they were all wrong in what they told me. Besides, there was something nasty about them.'

'Why should Her Majesty be interested in such things?' Sheena asked.

'Because . . .' Mary Stuart stopped. 'I suppose because she is Italian,' she finished quickly.

Sheena felt it was an evasive answer and not quite the

truth. Mary Stuart thought there was another reason for the Queen's preoccupation, but at the moment she was not going to tell her what it was.

'It was very, very kind of her to give me this gown,' Sheena said earnestly, feeling that some expression of loyalty was required of her and yet not quite certain why she must be so positive about it.

'Of course it was,' Mary Stuart agreed. 'I wonder if the stars or the crystal suggested it? Or was it her own idea?'

'I think it was her own idea,' Sheena asserted loyally.

'More than likely,' Mary Stuart said. 'More than likely. And I do not suppose it will be long before you find out the reason for it!'

Sheena longed to ask her more, but she knew it was useless. Then she thought there was only one person who would tell her the truth—the Duc. But with a toss of her head she told herself she would not humiliate herself by asking him questions.

5

As Sheena came from the apartments of Mary Stuart a gentleman approached her.

'May I introduce myself, Ma'mselle?' he asked with an elaborate bow. 'I am the Marquess de Maupré and Her Majesty, Queen Catherine, has requested that we become acquainted.'

Sheena curtsied, thinking that he was one of the best-looking men she had ever seen. She then corrected the impression, as she realised he was older than she thought and there was something slightly repellent, although she could not explain what it was, about his smile.

'Her Majesty has spoken of you so warmly,' he went on. 'In fact, she told me that I must look for one of the loveliest young women I had ever beheld, so that it was not difficult to recognise you on sight.'

Sheena dropped her eyes. She had an instinctive distrust of those who paid very fulsome compliments. Although she had now been at the French Court for over two weeks, she still found it difficult not to blush and look confused when she received unstinted admiration expressed in the flowery, extravagant language which was the fashion amongst the Court gallants.

'Her Majesty is very kind,' she murmured.

'She is more than that,' the Marquess replied. 'She has your welfare very deeply at heart, Ma'mselle.'

Sheena looked surprised. She was already extremely grateful to the Queen for the lovely gowns she had sent her. Nevertheless, she still found it difficult to imagine why Queen Catherine should sing'e her out for so much favour unless it was to show her devotion to the little Queen of Scotland.

It was with a slight sense of perplexity that she heard the Marquess continue:

'Her Majesty is right. We are, indeed, fortunate that you should choose to visit us from your country so far away in the North. And yet to me you look more like the sunshine and warmth of our southern shores rather than the bleak, windy coldness of the North.'

'People are usually mistaken about Scotland,' Sheena said quickly in defence of her beloved country. 'It is, indeed, very cold in the winter, but in the summer it can be warm and sunny and ever since I was a child I have bathed in the North Sea.'

'If only I could see you,' the Marquess murmured. 'You must look like Aphrodite rising from the waves.'

Sheena turned away a little impatiently. This sort of compliment bored her. She knew the ladies at Court revelled in listening to their praises, put on, as her old nanny would have said, 'with a bucket of butter'. And yet she felt sometimes as if the insincerity of it all would make her cry out in protest at the scented, effeminate young men who had nothing else to do but write verses about emotions she was quite sure they were incapable of feeling.

'Your pardon, Monsieur,' she said to the Marquess, 'but I have things to do, so if you will excuse . . .'

He interrupted her.

'No, no, do not go,' he pleaded. 'I must talk to you. It is of the utmost import.'

There was no doubting that his tone seemed urgent and sincere, so she let him lead her to one of the seats along the corridor placed beside a window overlooking the formal garden.

'As I have already said, Her Majesty has spoken of you so warmly that I felt that you could not help but return a little of her affection,' he said.

Sheena glanced at him quickly and then looked out towards the garden. She had been long enough at the Court by now to realise that under the fulsome polite surface of the compliments and courtesy there existed a bitter and vengeful battle-ground. Those who served the Queen loathed with a fanatical hatred the beautiful Duchesse de Valentinois, who, it was quite obvious, held the King in the hollow of her hand.

She might be eighteen years older than Henri: she might have long passed her fiftieth year; but she was still undoubtedly the most beautiful woman in France and without any question at all she was the most powerful.

Sheena, ready to condemn the illicit liaison because of the Puritanical manner in which she had been brought up and the strict standards of morality which prevailed in her father's house and in those of his friends, found it difficult not to admire the Duchesse for the brilliant way in which she handled everybody and everything, including the King himself.

Everything in her part of the Palace, everything that appertained to the State and Government of the people with whom she came in contact, ran smoothly and efficiently. Sheena would have been very stupid indeed if she had not realised that the statesmen and the politicians, when they left the Duchesse's presence, were satisfied and ready to go on serving the King with a loyalty which could not have been extracted from them if they had not known that the policy propounded to them was both right and just.

'She is a great woman,' she heard the Cardinal say to an ancient and venerable courtier with a long beard.

'She is more than that,' the old man replied almost beneath his breath. 'She is a great Queen.'

The Cardinal had not contradicted him but smiled, and Sheena, who had been standing near them and overheard the conversation, moved away puzzled and perplexed.

How could the Church, she wondered, recognise anything so wrong and illegal as the Duchesse's relationship with the King?

And yet the longer she stayed at the Palace, the more she realised how hopelessly ineffectual the Queen herself managed to be. She seldom came out of her apartments; and when she did the contrast between her dowdy appearance and the elegance and freshness of the King's mistress was almost farcical. As for conversation, the Queen's only enthusiasm was for the predictions and prophecies of her astrologers and necromancers.

Sheena learnt that the Duchesse rode every morning as soon as dawn broke; that she bathed dai'y in cold water and ate very sparingly of the rich dishes which loaded the King's table.

The Queen, on the contrary, took no exercise. She was growing fat and her skin was very sallow. She ate enormously and it was often obvious to the most impartial observer that she was sadly in need of a bath.

'Nevertheless, she is his true wife,' Sheena had told herself, not once but a dozen times, in an effort to convince herself that her sympathy must lie with the Queen.

'You are too young to contend with the intrigues of Palaces,' the Marquess was saying in her ear, and with a jerk she brought her thoughts back and tried to listen to what he was saying.

'I am not concerned with the Palace or its intrigues,' Sheena answered sharply. 'I am here to serve Mary Queen of Scotland, my own Queen, and frankly I am interested in nothing e'se.'

'But your own Queen is to be our Queen too,' the Marquess said. 'And therefore you cannot help but realise the dangers and difficulties which lie ahead.'

He glanced over his shoulder as if to be sure no one was listening.

'What has that arch-witch said to you?' he asked in a low voice.

Sheena opened her eyes wide.

'I do not know of whom you are speaking.'

'I think you do,' he replied. 'Who but the woman who has bewitched and enslaved the King? Are you not sorry for him? A young man caught in the web of a very old but very wily spider.'

'I imagine the King can look after himself,' Sheena answered coldly.

'On the contrary,' the Marquess contradicted. 'A man is always wax in the hands of a clever woman, and the King had no chance. She ensnared him when he was but a babe in the cradle. When he was a little boy she accompanied him on the fateful journey to Spain, when he and his brother were sent there as hostages to be bullied and ill treated. Heaven knows what wiles she used to make him remember her, but on his return he went to her side and has never left her since.'

Sheena said nothing. She was wondering what purpose the Marquess had in telling her all this, most of which she knew already.

'Cannot you understand,' the Marquess said in a little above a whisper, 'that he must be saved—saved for the sake of France?'

'How can that concern me?' Sheena enquired.

'Perhaps you wi'l find a way where we have failed,' the Marquess replied. 'Talk to him. Let him realise there are other women in the world besides the Duchesse. You are young, you are gay, you look like spring itself. Bring a little sunshine into his life—young, dancing sunshine—and dim the last gleam of the old sun which should long since have set.'

Sheena gazed at him with a sudden distaste.

'I think, *Monsieur Le Marquess*,' she said coldly, 'that it would be far better if I did not concern myself with things outside my special duties.'

She rose as she spoke, holding herself stiff and upright, but conscious of how much taller he was than she and that her voice trembled a little from nervousness. He too rose to his feet.

'The Queen will be distressed,' he said. 'I think she relied on your sympathy and your understanding of her almost intolerable situation. She is very lonely and without many friends.'

Sheena's heart was touched. She could never bear to think of anyone being unhappy.

'I assure you, Monsieur,' she replied quickly, 'that I am deeply grateful to Her Majesty for her kindness to me, for the beautiful gowns she has given me and the fact that she has invited me several times to her apartments. I would not have her think me ungrateful.'

'That is all I think she asks of you,' the Marquess said. 'A little gratitude and perhaps a little friendliness. May I tell Her Majesty that you will call on her this afternoon at half past three?'

'I will endeavour to do so,' Sheena answered, 'unless my own Queen should require my presence.'

'I feel sure that Queen Catherine can rely on you,' the Marquess said.

He paused. Sheena curtsied and moved away. As she turned she had a last glimpse of his face and she had the feeling that he was somehow pleased with the way the interview had gone rather than, as she had expected, being cast down and annoyed at her uncompromising attitude.

What did it all mean? she asked herself. Why had he chosen to talk to her? And why had he been so insistent on her placing herself on the Queen's side in the battle between the two most important women in the country?

It was all ridiculous, she thought. What could she do one way or the other? She did not want to take sides, and, apart from that, she could not help but feel, although it was wrong to do so, that the Queen must be in many ways to blame for having lost her husband to the beautiful and clever Duchesse.

She thought the same later in the day as she walked through the Palace to the Queen's apartments. Where the Duchesse ruled there was freshness, open windows and great vases of fragrant flowers. The Queen's part of the Palace was airless, dusty with incense and other strange, haunting perfumes which made Sheena feel uneasy. There were no flowers, only a mass of lighted tapers even in the daytime.

The Queen was wearing a mass of jewels, badly chosen and ill assorted, so that it was difficult to admire them because they detracted one from another. Her gown was embroidered, too, and it seemed over-fussy after the c'assical beauty of the Duchesse's white-and-black dresses, which were not only exquisitely made but absolutely spotless.

The Queen was alone with her favourite lady-in-waiting, seated by a big fire which made the room almost unbearably hot. Sheena curtsied low and the Queen put out a hand and laid it on her shoulder.

'I am glad to see you, child. The Marquess said he was not quite certain whether you would come, but I was hoping that you would contrive to leave your young mistress for a short while so that we could get better acquainted.'

'Your Majesty is very gracious,' Sheena answered, trying not to think even to herself that the Queen's hand was too heavy for her age and that the huge dish of sweetmeats by her side was responsible for the rolls of fat under her chin. She had given birth to her tenth child nearly a

71

year ago and her figure was ungainly and misshapen from the frequent pregnancies.

'Be seated, Mistress McCraggan,' the Queen commanded. 'I wish to talk with you.'

Sheena seated herself nervously on a low chair.

'The Marquess has told me of the kind things you have said about me,' the Queen went on. 'I am touched that someone from so far away should understand so clearly all that I suffer and endure in this great Palace which is really little more than a prison.'

Sheena looked startled. The Marquess, she thought wryly, must have embroidered very considerably anything she had actually said and have invented the rest.

The Queen clasped her hands together.

'Ah, Mistress McCraggan, I am so unhappy, so miserable. In fact, if it were not for my dear, devoted friend here'—she indicated her lady-in-waiting—'I would often wish myself dead.'

'No, Madame, you must not say that,' Sheena protested. 'You have so much to live for.'

'What have I to live for?' the Queen asked. 'My children? The Duchesse de Valentinois chooses their nurses and their tutors; she directs the Royal kitchens to serve only the food she considers good for them. I am not allowed to interfere in anything. The moment my baby is born she takes charge of it; in fact it becomes hers.'

The Queen spoke with such bitterness that Sheena could not help feel a pang of sympathy for the unfortunate woman. Impulsively she put out her hand.

'Your Majesty! We would all help you if we could.'

'It is witchcraft!' the Queen said, dropping her voice to a low, sibilant whisper. 'Witchcraft! She is old, but the devil has made her young. Where are her wrinkles? Where is the thickening of her body, the greying of her hair? Only witchcraft can keep age at bay and the fact that the devil himself possesses her soul.'

Sheena took a deep breath. She did not believe in such things. They were nonsense, of course, and yet it was hard

72

not to feel there must be something in what the Queen said.

'Sometimes,' the Queen continued, 'I have felt the King groping towards me like a child who is afraid of the dark. Yet always, before I can speak, before he can free himself even for a few seconds from her spell, she pulls him back. He has gone and I am left alone with only fear and misery as my companions.'

Sheena did not know what to say. She had never expected that the Queen would confide in her and she felt that any words of consolation would sound either inadequate or impertinent. The Queen gave a deep sigh.

'I try not to talk of my unhappiness,' she said. 'I must try to bear my own burdens and not lay them on other shoulders. But you? You will think of me with kindness?'

'Of course, Your Majesty,' Sheena said eagerly. 'And if I could help you I would.'

'You would?'

The Queen's eyes suddenly brightened. There was a look of excitement in them.

'Yes, of course I would,' Sheena repeated.

She did not know why, but she wished she had not given such a promise.

'I will remember that. You are my friend, my dear, kind friend,' the Queen said.

She held out her hand, and Sheena, realising what was expected of her, dropped on one knee to kiss it.

It was at that moment that the door was flung open and a flunkey announced:

'His Majesty the King, Your Majesty!'

The Queen rose to her feet.

'Oh, Sire, you have come!' she exclaimed.

The King walked quickly into the room. He was, Sheena noticed, wearing his characteristic expression of moroseness and gloom. He seldom looked anything else unless the Duchesse was with him. It was difficult to believe that he was not much older than his thirty-eight years.

'Well, what is it?' he asked uncompromisingly.

He stood in the centre of the room looking at the Queen

in a manner which Sheena felt had something hostile about it. And then as she did not speak he added:

'You sent for me. I understood it was important.'

'It is, indeed,' the Queen said. 'But first, have you no word of greeting for Mistress Sheena McCraggan?'

The King seemed to notice Sheena for the first time.

'Ah, indeed! Our visitor from Scotland,' he exclaimed, 'I hope, Ma'mselle, that you are enjoying yourself.'

'I am glad of the opportunity to serve my own Queen, Sire,' Sheena answered.

'Our cousin and future daughter-in-law. Mary Stuart is a beautiful and charming child and we love her dearly. Is that not so?' he questioned, turning to his wife.

The Queen nodded.

'Mary Stuart has won all our hearts,' she smiled. 'And especially yours, Sire. There is something attractive about these girls from Scotland which draws all men to them like magnets. Look at Mistress McCraggan. I have been telling her that with that perfect skin, clear as a mountain stream, and hair that seems to imprison the sunbeams, she will have to be very careful to keep the young gallants of your Court at arm's length.'

Sheena stared at the Queen in astonishment. Her Majesty had said none of these things and she could not imagine why she should wish to invent such lies. She looked back at the King and found he was watching her with a faint smile on his lips.

'She is beautiful, is she not?' the Queen asked.

As the King did not answer, she turned to Sheena and added, as if in explanation:

'His Majesty has a great eye for beauty. Many of our Court painters ask him to choose a model for them rather than trust their own judgment.'

Sheena dropped her eyes so that the Queen should not see the expression in them. She was well aware that whenever the King commissioned a picture, a sculpture or a piece of enamel, the model was always the same—the Duchesse de Valentinois.

'We must make Mistress McCraggan happy, as she has come such a long way to be our guest,' the Queen continued. 'Perhaps Your Majesty will dance with her one evening. See how tiny her feet are. She should move like a feather across the floor.'

'We must see, we must see,' the King replied. 'And now, my dear, if we could discuss the reason why you sent for me I should be obliged. I have three gentlemen waiting for me on the tennis-court.'

'Yes, yes, of course,' the Queen said.

She glanced at the lady-in-waiting, who made a gesture which Sheena understood and they both sank to the ground in a deep curtsy and backed towards the door.

'Such youth! Such grace!' Sheena heard the Queen breathe as the door shut behind them.

Outside the lady-in-waiting gave Sheena a sour look.

'You can go now,' she said, and turned away abruptly.

Sheena hurried down the long gallery feeling like a child released from school. It was only when she reached the other end of the Palace that she realised that she had hurried unnecessarily quickly and that her cheeks were flushed.

She rounded a corner and found a bevy of people advancing towards her. In the centre of them was Mary Stuart with the Dauphin by her side, saying something in a gay, excited voice which brought a ripple of laughter from the dozen or so young people of the same age who escorted them. Behind came the Duchesse de Valentinois and the Duc de Salvoire.

'Sheena, we have been looking for you!' Mary Stuart cried. 'Where have you been hiding yourself?'

'I am sorry if you should have wanted me, Ma'am,' Sheena replied, curtsying.

'Of course I wanted you,' Mary Stuart answered. 'I could not think where you had hidden yourself. I even imagined you might have been kidnapped.'

'I am quite safe and sound, I assure you,' Sheena smiled.

'Then come along with us at once,' Mary Stuart commanded. 'We are going to see a new juggler who has just arrived from Italy. They say he is phenomenal and can keep twenty balls in the air at the same time.'

Laughing and arguing whether such a thing was possible, the young people hurried on. When they reached one of the narrow staircases which led to the ground floor of the Palace, Sheena found herself at the back of the party and stood aside to let the Duchesse de Valentinois go first.

She smiled at Sheena, thanked her and moved down the stairs talking animatedly to a small, dark man who Sheena recognised as the Ambassador from Portugal. Then with a sudden little thump of her heart she realised that the Duc was at her side looking down at her with an expression on his face which she was certain was one of disapproval.

'Where have you been?'

Only she could hear the question. Just for a moment she was frightened and then some of her Scottish pride came to her rescue and she asked herself what business it was of his?

'Why should you be interested?' she enquired, looking up at him defiantly. She thought his eyes were more cynical than ever as he replied.

'I have my reasons for asking.'

'Perhaps I have my reasons for refusing to tell you,' she countered.

'I do not believe that it was an assignation if that is what you are trying to pretend,' he said. 'Gustave de Cloude, at any rate, had no idea where you might be.'

If he was intending to annoy her he succeeded.

Sheena tossed her head.

'What has the Comte got to do with it?' she laughed.

'I think only you can answer that question,' the Duc rep'ied.

They went down a few more steps before he spoke again.

'Are you not going to tell me?' he asked.

'Why should I?' she replied.

Quite unexpectedly his hand came out. She felt his fingers on her arm.

'Do not be a little fool,' he said. 'What you are doing is dangerous.'

Just for a moment Sheena felt unable to move. Then impatiently she shook herself free of his hand.

'I do not know what you mean,' she told him. 'I am not doing anything dangerous or otherwise. I just do not see why I should be questioned and cross-examined.'

'Perhaps I am trying to help you,' the Duc said.

'I doubt it,' Sheena replied. 'I do not believe you would he'p anyone without an ulterior motive.'

Even as she spoke she knew she was being rude and would have bitten back the words because they were undignified and childish. Why, she asked herself, did this man always have the effect of making her feel on the defensive, of making her want to fight him? It had been war the very first moment they met and now it was war again. She threw all caution to the winds.

'Leave me alone,' she said angrily. 'I do not want to be embroiled in intrigues, yours or anyone else's.'

It seemed to her there was surprisingly an expression of relief on his face.

'I wish I could be sure of that,' he said quietly.

'Well, you can be,' Sheena snapped. 'All I want to do is to serve my Queen.'

'And you can do that best,' the Duc said, 'by not becoming embroi'ed in other factions of the Court.'

Angrily Sheena stamped her foot.

'I am not becoming embroiled,' she cried. 'Why do you talk as if I were?'

'Because I do not think you know what you are doing,' he answered.

Exasperatedly Sheena replied:

'I am doing nothing. Cannot you understand that? Nothing at all.'

'Then where were you just now?'

'Not anywhere that you might imagine,' Sheena answered hastily, feeling as if he had set a trap for her and she had somehow fallen into it.

'Then if you are not ashamed of it tell me where you were.'

'I was with the Queen,' she said defiantly. 'Is there anything wrong in that?'

'Alone?'

The question was shot at her like an arrow from a bow.

'Not the whole of the time.'

'Then who else?'

They had almost reached the bottom of the stairs and now Sheena looked up into his eyes, intending to defy him or perhaps tease him further. Then suddenly compelled by the authority that she saw there she was forced into telling him the truth.

'The King came in.'

She felt the Duc's sudden tension. She saw his lips part as if he was about to say something, but before he could speak, before she could know whether he was surprised or affected in any way by what she had said, the Duchesse de Valentinois turned round and her voice interrupted them.

'Do hurry, your Grace, or there will be no time for the performance,' she pleaded. 'The King will have finished his game of tennis and I shall be prevented from seeing the marvels of this new entertainer.'

The Duc stepped from Sheena's side.

'I will go ahead,' he said respectfully to the Duchesse, 'and see that everything is in readiness.'

'Please do that,' the Duchesse replied with a smile. 'You know that I cannot keep the King waiting.'

The Duc moved away and the Duchesse, still with a smile on her lips, turned to Sheena.

'I do not think, Mistress McCraggan, that you have met Señor Vermellio,' she said.

The Ambassador bowed. Sheena curtsied and then they were moving on down the corridor and the Duc was already out of sight.

While the others applauded, laughed and praised the

78

juggler, Sheena found it difficult to concentrate on anything but her own thoughts. What had the Duc meant? she wondered. What was the danger? Why had he questioned her as to who else was with the Queen? Had he suspected that she had not told the truth or was there someone else whom he thought she might meet there?

It was all so puzzling and because such thoughts worried her she was almost glad when Comte Gustave de Cloude crossed the room to sit by her side.

They had long ago made up their differences of that first morning when Sheena had gone to talk with him in the gardens and had run away because he frightened her.

She realised now how stupid she had been, first in accepting his invitation, which had been given light-heartedly with every expectation that she would refuse, and secondly in being frightened or upset by his expressions of devotion.

She knew by now that every woman in the Palace expected a man to make love to her if they were left alone for even a few moments—and even when they were not. Love, of one sort or another, was the whole conversation in the French Court and Sheena longed sometimes for a strong, gusty wind from the North Sea to blow about them all and make them think of something less emotional.

'You are looking serious,' the Comte said now. 'What is troubling you?'

'Nothing,' Sheena answered. 'And please do not ask me questions. I am tired of being questioned. I just want to creep into a hole and hope that no one will notice me.'

'That is impossible,' Gustave de Cloude said, and Sheena held up her hand in warning.

'Do not say it,' she said. 'You promised, no compliments.'

'What a strange girl you are,' he said. 'I cannot think of any woman, young or old, who does not want to be told she is lovely, attractive and desirable, especially when she is overwhelmingly all three.'

'That is a fine!' Sheena exclaimed. 'You have broken our pact.'

79

He laughed and fished in his purse for a gold coin.

'Here you are, then,' he said. 'The fine is almost worth it.'

Sheena took the coin from him. After he had apologised for his behaviour in the garden they had come to an arrangement that if he paid her compliments he should be fined for them and the money would go to the Little Sisters of the Poor who worked in the worst parts of Paris. Already Sheena had been able to send them quite a considerable sum of money; and now, as she took the gold coin from him, she said somewhat dubiously:

'You can afford this, can you not?'

'I assure you I am a very rich and very eligible young man.'

'Then why do you not get married?'

'Because until now I have never seen anyone who really attracted me,' he answered.

Again she held up a warning finger, knowing as she did so that he was, in actual fact, falling in love with her.

'It is only because I keep him at a distance,' she told herself. At the same time, she could not help liking, with something nearly akin to affection, the gay, impulsive young gallant who came from one of the best families in France and who she had discovered, underneath the fashionable affectations of the time, was kind and understanding and unexpectedly considerate.

'All right, I will not tease you,' he said now. 'But you looked so serious that I was worried, that is why I came to sit beside you. Is there anything I can do?'

It was like him, Sheena thought, to offer his services. She turned to smile at him warmly and as she did so saw the Duc's eyes fixed on her. She felt herself shiver almost as if, as the saying was, a ghost walked over her grave.

'What is it?' Gustave asked. 'You must let me help.'

'I do not know. It is nothing I can put into words,' Sheena said. 'It is only an instinct, something that is happening that I do not understand.'

'Tell me about it,' he pleaded.

'There is nothing to tell,' Sheena answered. 'When there is . . .'

He interrupted.

'Promise that you will let me help; promise.'

'I promise,' Sheena said. 'I do know I can trust you.'

'Do you mean that?' He turned towards her eagerly. 'Sheena, I must say it. Let me say it now. Let me say it whatever it may cost me in charity. I love you! I love you really, with my whole heart. Will you marry me?'

She shook her head and as she did so glanced sideways and saw that the Duc was still watching her.

'Danger! Danger!'

She could still hear his voice saying it and she felt a sudden panic sweep over her because she did not understand.

6

There came a discreet knock at the door. Maggie crossed the room and opened it. Sheena heard her mutter something and then she closed the door again.

' 'Tis the messenger,' she said in a low voice.

Sheena raised her head from her writing-desk.

'I have nearly finished,' she said dubiously, and sat biting at the end of her quill, her mind filled with indecision and worry.

What could she say to her father? She had been told that a messenger was leaving secretly for Scotland that night and that any letters she sent by his hand would be safe and not opened or spied on, as were all the other letters which left the Palace.

If Sheena had not suspected the presence of spies who watched everything and everybody, Maggie would soon have enlightened her.

'There's them that spies for the Queen,' she said. 'And

them that spies for the Duchesse. And there's the spies of the Church and the spies of the State. And besides all these there's a whole host of people who, as far as I can understand, spies for themselves.'

Maggie's tone was full of scorn, for like all decent, law-abiding folk she had a deep-rooted contempt for those who intrigued or approached any problem except in the most straightforward manner.

Sheena had wondered uneasily what Maggie would say if she knew the instructions she herself had received from her father before she left Scotland. How easy, in theory, it had seemed then to find out the things he wanted. How absolutely impossible it was in practice.

Her first letters had been guarded and deliberately without any information which might be construed not only as a criticism of the French Court but even that she was taking sides.

Now, in this letter, she had told him many of the difficulties. And yet even to her father it was impossible to write all the truth. How could she hurt him by saying: *Our little Queen has almost forgotten Scotland and, indeed, has little interest in what goes on there?*

Perhaps because she was so anxious to hide this, of all things, from him she became more verbose than she need have been about other people at the Court.

The Duc de Salvoire, she wrote, *is always in attendance on the Duchesse de Valentinois. He is a hard, cynical, rude man who likes people to fear him and who, I feel, would be utterly ruthless as an enemy.*

That disposed of the Duc. She then described the kindness of the Queen in giving her such beautiful clothes and went on:

The Queen is quiet and unobtrusive, she looks, as I heard one courtier put it, as if she were 'a hungry cat'. However, I think that they all underestimate her and she

82

seems to me far more like a sleeping panther who might one day awaken.

Sheena read what she had written and wondered almost why she had said it. Did she really think that about the Queen? The words seemed to have dropped from her pen without her conscious volition.

A sleeping panther! Why should she think that? She thought of those bright inquisitive eyes, which would be veiled as the Queen deliberately sank into the background, and when she allowed the Duchesse de Valentinois to precede her even on important occasions. And yet sometimes Sheena had seen a tightening of her lips, a little pulse beating in her thick, short neck; and she suspected that the Queen was not so complaisant as she appeared.

What else could she say? How else could she keep him from realising how little she had written about Mary Stuart?

The Marquess de Maupré is charming, she scribbled. *He quite rightly supports the Queen and yet I think no one could fail to like him. He is agreeable and charming to everyone and excellent company when there is a party.*

There came another knock at the door.

'The messenger is impatient,' Maggie said.

Hastily Sheena finished off the letter. She had the feeling that her father would be annoyed at so much triviality and detail without any of the facts that he had hoped to hear from her. Yet what else could she do?

She realised suddenly that she had always been afraid of her father. He had shown her little love since her mother died, but had always been too busy with affairs of State to spend much time at home. He was used to giving commands and he had ordered her to go to France and find out all she could about the King's intentions towards Scotland and the placing of Mary Stuart on the Throne of England.

What an impossible task it was! How could she help but

fail him? She smiled a little ruefully as she handed the letter, sealed it with a ring which bore the McCraggan crest and holding it for a moment against her heart said aloud:

'I only wish I could go with this letter. Our rightful place is in Scotland, Maggie.'

'That it is,' Maggie agreed whole-heartedly. 'We're like two bits o' purp'e heather trying to grow on a foreign soil which dinna ken how to nourish us.'

'They are kind, very kind, here,' Sheena said. 'But I have a longing for the mountains and the burns running down into the sea, and the mist in the morning and the absolute quiet at night.'

'Ye're right,' Maggie agreed, her voice suddenly hoarse with emotion. 'Palaces are not the places for us.'

Suddenly remembering that the messenger was still waiting, Sheena hurried to the door. She pulled it open. Outside was a small, wizened little man with deep lines running from his nose to the corners of his down-turned mouth. His small beady eyes peered at her from a network of wrinkles.

Sheena was start'ed by the sight of him. She did not know what she had expected, but she had not imagined the messenger would be so old.

'Is it you who is going to Scotland?' she asked in French.

'*Oui, Ma'mselle*, I leave tonight.'

'But . . . but why?' Sheena asked.

He looked at her sourly.

'That's my business,' he replied. 'Is the letter ready? It'll cost you a louis for me to take it there.'

Maggie had the money ready. Sheena took it from her hand and gave it to the man before she handed over the letter. She had a sudden reluctance to part with what she had written. Then feeling she was being absurd she gave him the letter and he placed it in his doublet.

Without a word he turned on his hee' and walked away down the passage and she saw as he left her that his legs were rather bowed as if he had spent too much of his life in the saddle.

'Who is he?' Sheena asked as she re-entered her bed-chamber and shut the door. 'What do you know about him?'

'They say he is trustworthy enough,' Maggie answered.

'I hope so, indeed,' Sheena said sharply. 'I would not wish that letter of mine to fall into any hands except those of my father.'

Maggie said nothing and Sheena knew that they were both thinking the same thing. It was hard in a strange country to know who was trustworthy and who was not.

As if she was afraid to say more, Sheena walked across the room to stare at her reflection in the burnished mirror. She was wearing yet another gown which the Queen had given her, of pale-blue satin looped with silver ribbons, and it made her look very young and her skin more dazzlingly transparent than ever.

She stared for a moment at her reflection. Instead of seeing herself she saw her father's face, puckered and anxious, his brows knit as he tried to read between the lines she had written him and find some answer to the questions with which his nob'es and the Elders would be sure to ply him once they learned he had heard from France.

'I am failing him,' Sheena thought miserably and on an impulse turned towards the door.

'Where are you going?' Maggie asked.

'I am going to try and talk to the King,' Sheena answered. 'It is something I ought to have done long ago.'

She swept through the door and down the passage, knowing that at this hour of the afternoon the King was likely to be found in one of the great salons receiving Ambassadors and other notabilities in audience. There would be no possibility of talking to him then, Sheena thought, but later he would slip away for a game of tennis and then there was always the chance of intercepting him. Even so, she realised it wou'd be a formidable, if not impossible, task to get him alone.

'Where are you going, looking so proud and disdainful?' she heard a voice call after her and she turned to see that intent in her own thoughts she had passed the Marquess de Maupré who had come into the passage from another staircase.

'I . . . I was wondering where everyone was . . . hiding.'

He smiled at her. He was, she thought, even more handsome, more debonair, than usual, in a doublet of white velvet slashed with crimson satin and ornamented with diamonds and rubies.

'I think you will find "everyone", as you put it, is in the garden,' the Marquess replied. 'The King is due to play tennis in half-an-hour's time and your own Queen has challenged the Dauphin to a game of battledore.'

'I must go and watch!' Sheena exclaimed.

'Do not fret yourself,' the Marquess smiled. 'I think I am the only person who has noticed your absence.'

Sheena laughed a little ruefully.

'That is not much of a compliment,' she complained.

She was being coquettish, for she had learned since her arrival at the French Court that women were expected to flirt rather than talk, and now she glanced at the Marquess from under her eyelashes without really thinking of what she was doing.

He bent nearer towards her.

'You are enchanting,' he said in a low voice.

'I am convinced that you say that to every woman,' Sheena replied almost automatically. At the same time she wondered why her heart did not flutter because he was so devastatingly handsome.

'I speak the truth,' he protested. 'But, alas, I cannot hope to be the only person who admires you. There is someone else who extols your praises at all times and arouses in me a jealousy such as I have never felt before.'

'I do not believe a word of it,' Sheena answered, but all the same she could not help being interested.

At first she had been repelled by the fulsome compliments of the courtiers, but now she had grown used to them and she was honest enough to admit to herself that it was fun to be flattered by such a handsome man. It was also exciting to be told one was attractive—not once but a hundred times a day by the look in every Frenchman's eyes, who had all been taught to look at a woman as if they really saw her and not just to treat her as a provider of food or a regrettable necessity.

How often had she seen her father glance up impatiently when she came into the room? How often had she noticed that he and his friends stopped talking or changed the subject because she was present? And as for compliments —they were far too intent on national problems and the exigencies of war to have time for anything so frivolous as complimenting a woman on her looks.

'Are you not curious?'

She realised that the Marquess was looking at her mouth in a manner which told her all too clearly where his thoughts were leading, and instinctively she moved a little further away from him and asked quickly:

'Curious about what?'

'About this person who admires you even more than I do and who says when you are not present such charming things about you that your cheeks as well as your ears should be burning a dozen times a day.'

'I cannot imagine who it could be,' Sheena answered. 'I know very few people well enough to think that they should even speak of me.'

'Then let me tell you who it is,' the Marquess said.

He put out his arms as he spoke and drew her close to him. Then with his lips close against her ear he whispered:
' 'Tis the King! '

Sheena looked up at him with incredulous eyes, then gave a little, uncertain laugh.

'Now I know you are teasing me,' she said. 'The King has hardly noticed me since I came here.'

'That is what you think,' the Marquess said. 'But the King is very shy. You do not know how reserved he has been ever since he was a child and was incarcerated in the Spanish prison and brutally ill treated by his jailors.'

'I have heard how miserable he was,' Sheena agreed.

'It has made it impossible for him to express himself,' the Marquess said, 'except when he is alone with a few old friends like myself. To women he appears tongue-tied and morose.'

'I think the King has eyes for only one woman,' Sheena said.

'You mean the Duchesse?' the Marquess enquired. 'She is old. Did you not know that she was eighteen years old when the King was born? Though he loved her for many years she has now become a habit. She makes things very comfortable for him. What man does not appreciate that? But his heart is free of her. I have known that for a long time.'

'I do not think such things are any concern of mine,' Sheena said crushingly.

She felt uncomfortable at the way the conversation was going and wished now that she had not lingered with the Marquess.

'Is it no concern of yours,' the Marquess asked softly, 'that the most important man in the civilised world is at your feet? He loves you, Sheena! He loves you!'

There was something in the way he said it, something in his voice, which frightened Sheena.

'You lie!' she said hotly, turning on him with a sudden blaze of fire in her eyes so that the Marquess took a step backwards before he realised what he was doing.

'You lie!' she repeated. 'And even if it was the truth I would not wish to hear it. The King is a married man— married to Queen Catherine—and I would despise any man, whoever he might be, who deserted the woman to whom he was joined both by the Church and State, for another.'

She almost shouted the words at him, and then before he could reply, before he could recover from the astonishment of her attack, she turned and marched away down the corridor, her small shoulders squared, her little head held high.

The Marquess made no attempt to follow her. He watched her until she was out of sight and then the expression of astonishment slowly left his face and he smiled, not a particu'arly nice smile but one which might have given Sheena, had she seen it, reason to think.

As it was, she was angry enough. She had shut her eyes to a great many excesses at the Court, the immorality which took place quite blatantly amongst the courtiers and ladies-in-waiting, and she had even turned a deaf ear to the many stories with which Maggie tried to regale her. But that she herself should be mixed up in any way with such a sorry state of affairs was something she had never anticipated.

Even though, she told herself, it was only a wild fabrication on the part of the Marquess, it was still infuriating that he should think such things or even consider them worth repeating. Her Scottish pride was aroused and she told herself fiercely that she would not be involved in the sordid intrigues or the amorous philanderings of the Court.

And even if such a thing were true, the Marquess had no right to repeat it to her. If it were true! The question pulled her to a full stop. Could it be possible that the King was in love with her? If so, what should she do about it?

Just for a moment she hesitated and then she walked on with her head still held high. There was no chance of it being true, she told her uneasy conscience. But if it were, the only thing to do would be to ignore it, to pay no attention.

It seemed to her that it was the devil himself who whispered: 'If it is true, how easy it would be to find out what your father wishes to know. How easily, in that way, you could help Scotland.'

'No! No! No!'

Without realising what she was doing Sheena said the words aloud. Then, reaching the bottom of the stairs, she found herself suddenly precipitated into a band of young people in the midst of whom was Mary Stuart. She saw Sheena and held out her hand.

'Come with us, Sheena,' she cried, 'and be the umpire. I know I am going to win—I always do—but His Royal Highness has forced me to accept a handicap. It is not fair, I swear it is not!'

Laughing and chattering and not noticing that Sheena made no effort to answer her, the little Queen led the way into the garden followed by her young friends. The Dauphin, looking pale and sickly and more in need of rest than a game, walked beside her, but it was obvious that he had little to say and was content to listen to the gay, teasing voice of his fiancée.

They swept towards the lawns and suddenly Sheena felt a hand on her arm and a voice at her side say:

'Her Grace the Duchesse de Valentinois wishes to have a word with you, Mistress McCraggan.'

'The Duchesse?'

'Yes, in her apartments. I have been looking for you and your maid told me I would find you here.'

'Does she want me at once?' Sheena asked.

'At once,' the courtier answered.

Sheena detached herself from the gay throng. They did not notice her go and she turned back the way they had come accompanied by the grey-haired man who had come to fetch her.

He led her up to the first floor and she realised that this was a part of the Palace she had not visited before. The rooms were magnificent and they passed through several ante-chambers until they came to one where the grey-haired man stopped and knocked on the door.

'Entrez!'

He left her for a moment and then returned to open the door and beckon her in. Sheena found herself in a large room with long windows and a balcony overlooking the gardens of the Palace. There was a large four-poster bed skilfully draped and surmounted by a frieze of beautifully carved gold cupids.

As if it made her feel uncomfortable, Sheena averted her eyes from it, and the Duchesse, in a gown of white embroidered with black and white pearls, came across the room towards her. She smiled and Sheena curtsied as briefly as she dared. She could not help but feel hostile, although the Duchesse was so beautiful that it was hard not to excuse the King for a liaison that had lasted so many years.

'Ah, Mistress McCraggan—no, I think it would be more friendly if I call you Sheena,' the Duchesse said. 'I am glad you have come to see me. I have been wanting to talk to you for some time.'

She made a gesture towards a sofa placed by the window, and then, as she did so, there came a knock on a door to the other side of the bedchamber to which Sheena had entered. A maid entered and spoke to the Duchesse, who said impatiently:

'Oh, dear! I had forgotten that I had asked him to come this afternoon.' She turned to Sheena. 'You must forgive me, my dear, for a moment. The Court jeweller has brought a necklace for me to see. It is a very special present that the King has promised me for my birthday and so I cannot send him away. Will you forgive me and wait for just a few moments until I can return?'

'I am at your service, Madame,' Sheena said coldly.

The Duchesse moved with exquisite grace across the room and disappeared through the doorway. Alone, Sheena got to her feet and looked around. There were three pictures in the room all by great artists, and all had taken as their model for the central figure of their picture the Duchesse herself.

There was no mistaking her as Diana the Huntress, any more than one could fail to recognise her features on the glorious sculpture which stood in one corner of the room or on the pieces of enamel which decorated the mantelpiece. Wherever one looked, the lovely face which had captivated a King stared back at one.

Instinctively Sheena threw back her head and looked

up at the ceiling, expecting to see the Duchesse portrayed there amidst the heavily decorated plasterwork. There was no picture but instead the entwined arms, 'H' and 'D', with which the King, to commemorate his love, had adorned every Palace that he and his mistress had ever visited.

The cipher had been cleverly conceived, Sheena thought, and wondered if any woman had ever been loved so well and truly as Diane de Poitiers.

And then as she stared at the ceiling a curious thing happened. She noticed what appeared to her at first to be a dirty mark beside one of the plaster roses which encircled the cipher. She looked again and thought that a piece of the design had fallen from the ceiling.

Then with a'most a sick feeling of apprehension she realised that what she was looking at was an eye! An eye staring down at her from the ceiling; an eye which moved and which undoubtedly belonged to a human being.

She got to her feet and walked over to the window. Surely, she thought, she must have been mistaken. Then casually, because she did not wish to reveal what she had discovered, she glanced round the room again and then up at the ceiling. Yes, undoubtedly there was an eye watching her.

To whom could it belong? Who was there? Who dared to spy in such a manner on the Duchesse?

Sheena felt quite sick at the discovery. There was something horrible about it, something which made her want to run away. And then, as she stood there indecisive, her fingers twisted together in her agitation, the door through which she had entered the room opened and she looked round to see that the King stood there.

'Where is the Duchesse?' he asked, speaking for the moment as if she was a chambermaid, so quick and imperious was his tone.

'She . . . she is in the next room, Your Majesty,' Sheena replied.

As if the King suddenly remembered his manners he

smiled and said in a very different tone of voice:

' 'Tis Mistress McCraggan, is it not? I am afraid I did not recognise you for the moment. You say that the Duchesse is in the next room?'

'Yes, Sire.'

'Do you know with whom she is engaged?'

'Her Grace mentioned a jeweller, Your Majesty.'

'Why, yes, I know now who is there.'

He strode across the room and flung open the door which Sheena decided obviously led into the Duchesse's dressing-room. There was a sudden murmur of voices and then he, too, had disappeared, leaving Sheena alone again.

'I believe he was jealous,' she thought suddenly. 'I think he came back from the tennis-court to find the Duchesse because he hated playing without her being there to watch him.'

What rubbish the Marquess was talking—and, yet, how could she be sure? What a topsy-turvy world this was, with spies everywhere even with their eyes looking down from the ceiling!

Should she go? Sheena asked herse'f, or should she stay? She was still in an agony of indecision when the dressing-room door opened and the King came into the room again.

'The Duchesse will not be long now,' he told Sheena with almost a note of joyfulness in his voice. 'And then Her Grace promised that she will bring you to the tennis-courts.'

'I would not wish to incommode her Grace . . .' Sheena began, only to be hushed into silence by an imperious wave of the hand.

'That is what her Grace wishes,' he said. 'And who are we mere mortals to question her commands?'

He smiled at Sheena as he spoke and then suddenly she took courage. Let the spy above listen if he wanted to, she thought. This was her opportunity and she must take it.

'I wonder, Sire, if I might say something to you?' she began and in as low a voice as she dared.

93

'What is it?' the King asked, a little testily.

'Before I left Scotland, Your Majesty,' Sheena went on quickly, afraid that he would prevent her saying it, 'my father told me that Mary, Queen of England, was in ill health. She is not expected to live long. Should she die, they believe that the English will attempt to place her sister, Elizabeth, on the Throne.'

'She has no right to it,' the King said gruffly. 'No right at all. The French Crown Jurists have decreed that as Henry himself insisted that his marriage to Anne Boleyn was a union with no legal foundation this makes Elizabeth illegitimate and therefore not the rightful heir to the Throne of England.'

'Scotland thinks the same, Your Majesty,' Sheena said, 'and, of course, believes, as you do, that Mary Stuart should be crowned.'

'So she should. So she should,' the King said. 'And as my future daughter-in-law I shall insist that she shall be acknowledged Queen of England.'

'You will send arms and soldiers to fight for her?' Sheena asked a little breathlessly.

No one could fail to notice the way in which the King's manner changed. For the moment he did not speak and then in a very different tone of voice he said:

'I have already instructed our heralds to get out a design showing the entwined arms, the Royal Arms of England and Scotland surmounted by the Crown of France.'

'But supposing that the English offer the Throne to Elizabeth?' Sheena insisted.

The King turned away from her.

'Mary Tudor is not yet dead, my child,' he said. 'It may be the will of God that she will live for many years longer.'

With a sense of hopelessness Sheena watched him leave the room. He did not look back at her and although she curtsied she knew he was unaware of it. She was well aware, too, that she had achieved nothing by her conversation except the uneasy feeling within herself that what-

94

ever happened the King did not intend to fight for the little Queen of Scotland.

Perhaps he thought the questions coming from her had been just impertinent, Sheena thought to herse'f. And yet in her heart she knew almost as if she could see into the future, that while Henri II of France would proclaim his daughter-in-law to be the Queen of England he would not send ships, men and guns to place her on the Throne.

Sheena shut her eyes. She knew what a terrible blow this would be to the men planning and plotting in Scotland, not only for the Throne of England but to the survival of their own land.

'I must be wrong. Naturally he would not tell me any-thing,' she told herself. And yet some clairvoyance within her heart told her that she had stumbled upon the truth. She felt as if it was almost unbearable. She knew in that moment that her country had been deserted in an hour of need and there was nothing she could do about it.

Without thinking it might be rude, without wondering even what the Duchesse would feel about it, she turned and went blindly from the room, unconsciously retracing her steps towards her own apartments like a child who runs to cry out its misery in some familiar place.

She reached her own bedchamber. Maggie was still there sitting by the window sewing a gown that was a little too long in the bodice. She looked up in astonishment as Sheena came bursting into the room, shut the door behind her and stood leaning against it as if she had hardly the strength to carry herself across the room.

'What is the matter? What has happened?' Maggie enquired.

Sheena shook her head.

'Nothing, nothing at all,' she answered untruthfully.

She could not bring herself even to tell Maggie what she had just learned. Besides, she tried to reassure herself, it might not be true. Why should the King tell her, an in-significant child, his plans either for Scotland or Mary Stuart?

'There is something wrong,' Maggie insisted.

'No, no, it is nothing,' Sheena answered. 'I just felt tired and a little faint perhaps.'

'I will get you a glass of water,' Maggie said practically.

As she poured it out from a cut-glass bottle encrusted with the arms of France, Sheena forced herself to a state of composure.

'It must be the sudden heat,' she said, 'or perhaps I ran too fast up the stairs.'

For the first time she wondered what the Duchesse would think when she came back to find her gone. It was rude, terribly rude, to run away in such a manner. Quickly Sheena decided to make reparation.

'Maggie, will you go at once to the Duchesse de Valentinois's maid or lady-in-waiting and say that I apologise deeply for not waiting for her as she requested but I felt indisposed and am lying down on my bed?'

'The Duchesse de Valentinois! And what would ye be doing with her?' Maggie enquired.

'She asked to see me,' Sheena answered.

Maggie sniffed. It was the expression of a deeply respectable woman who was affronted by the licence in her own sex.

'I wonder what she wanted with me?' Sheena said. 'Perhaps now I shall never know.'

'From all I hear, if her Grace wants anything she'll get it sooner or later,' Maggie told her.

'I am sure that is true,' Sheena said. 'And, Maggie, do you by any chance know who has apartments on the second floor above the Duchesse? There are so many staircases and the Palace is built in such a strange way that I never know where I am, but I just wondered if you could find out.'

'There's no need to find out anything as simple as that,' Maggie replied. 'I ken well enough who is above the Duchesse's apartments. And plenty o' talk there is about it, I can tell ye, as to why those particular rooms were chosen.'

'Who occupies them?' Sheena asked.

'The Queen,' Maggie replied. 'And there's some say she could have had any room she liked to choose in any part of the Palace, but she demanded that floor and so the King, not to gainsay her, let her have her way.'

'She sleeps in the room above the Duchesse?' Sheena asked in a shocked voice.

'Exactly above,' Maggie replied a little grimly, watching Sheena's face.

7

Comte Gustave de Cloude was becoming insistent and Sheena, feeling it was more and more difficult to keep him at arm's length, slipped away from him through the formal gardens. She was escaping at the same time from the gay crowd of revellers who were dancing under the light of the summer moon augmented with a thousand fairy-lights hung amongst the trees and bushes.

It was a sight such as Sheena had never dreamed of seeing in the whole of her austere, quiet life in Scotland. Here, music and the chatter of voices seemed only part of the magic of flashing jewels, gowns of silk and satin and lace, and gentlemen so resplendent in their velvet doublets and glittering sword-hilts that Mary Stuart had declared they were 'like peacocks parading before us to show off their finery'.

It was the little Queen who had suggested this particular rout. Sheena had learned by now that any excuse served for a party or an assembly to amuse the jaded tastes of the Court and arouse enthusiasm amongst the bored courtiers who had far too little to do.

The King was always busy and so was the Duchesse de Valentinois on matters of State. But for the rest the days passed slowly with only intrigue, gossip and scandal to whet their appetites and to send the ladies-in-waiting or the gentlemen hurrying between the rival factions, ready to make trouble if only that it served to pass an idle hour.

But to Sheena, unused to luxury and certainly to the extravagance of a rich Court, everything was a delight— the silver and gold vessels which graced the table of the King; the flowers, the music from the most experienced orchestras and musicians in all France; the art treasures with which every room was decorated and embellished; and last of all the people themselves.

She could not help being fascinated by everyone. The quiet, meek Queen; the beautiful, all-powerful Duchesse; the reserved, almost sombre King over whom they fought an endless if undeclared battle. And most fascinating of all, as far as Sheena was concerned, was the little Queen of Scotland, whose marriage to the Dauphin it was now decided should take place next year.

Mary Stuart loved a party. She cou'd dance like a piece of thistledown and wanted always to take the lead in one way or another. Occasionally she recited poems in Latin or French and had delighted the King, but tonight she was dancing wildly with all the best-looking men at Court, and, Sheena had to add a little ruefully, flirting outrageously with them.

'If only I had her poise and confidence,' Sheena thought to herself for the hundredth time as she watched the chi'd to whom she had come out to be a guide and companion behaving like a woman three times her age and managing, without the least affectation, to be entrancing, desirable and coquettish all at once.

It was hard at these parties to keep track of anyone. All too soon Sheena found herself being pursued by Gustave de Cloude and finding it very difficult to think of anyone but him. He had had a great deal to drink, as had all the other young men, and soon she realised that un'ess she escaped from him all her prevarications and evasiveness of the last week or so would be undone.

This was not the hour of night, she decided, to plead

for friendliness; and so, when he was engaged in momentary conversation with the Comtesse René de Pouguet, who was glittering with jewels as she walked by on the arm of the Duc de Salvoire, Sheena slipped away.

It was quieter and not so brilliantly lit in the part of the gardens in which she found herself, but it seemed to her even more beautiful with the moon climbing high over the Pa'ace, casting a silver light on a fountain which flung a diamond cascade up towards the sable sky and let it fall down into the deep, curved bowl where goldfish swam amongst the water-lilies.

She stood watching the fountain for a little while and then she turned towards a rose-covered arbour where a marble seat was invitingly spread with silk cushions. She had almost reached it when out of the shadows stepped a man. His appearance was so unexpected that she gave a little startled gasp of fear before he spoke and she realised who he was.

'I have been watching you,' he said. 'You looked very lovely in the moonlight.'

The moonlight also made him appear more handsome than usual and as she curtsied to the Marquess de Maupré she wondered why he was alone here instead of being in attendance on some of the beautiful women grouped around the Queen and the Duchesse de Valentinois.

'I came to get my breath,' Sheena explained almost as if he had asked her why she was alone. 'There was such a crowd.'

'I think you were running away,' the Marquess said with a faint smile on his lips. 'I thought young Gustave de Cloude looked a little too possessive earlier in the evening.'

Sheena looked embarrassed. She had no desire to discuss the young Comte, whom she liked, with the Marquess.

'I think now I had better go back,' she said, hoping to end the conversation.

'There is no hurry,' the Marquess said. 'Sit down for a moment and tell me about yourself. We so seldom get the opportunity to be alone.'

Because she felt it would be rude and rather gauche to refuse point-blank, she seated herself as he suggested on the seat inside the arbour.

'I must not stop long,' she said primly. 'Her Majesty may be needing me.'

'The little Queen needed no one when I last saw her,' the Marquess said. 'If her expression was to be believed, she was having a most enjoyable time. But then she is, thank God, young enough to be able to enjoy herself and not be afraid to show it.'

'I think everyone must enjoy a party like this in such surroundings,' Sheena said.

'I wish that were true,' he replied. 'Unfortunately, most people are far too eaten up with enmity and malice to do anything but hate their neighbours.'

'Surely you are not cynical too?' Sheena said, and then blushed as she realised that she had been comparing him in her mind with the Duc de Salvoire.

'Who else is cynical?' the Marquess asked instantly.

Sheena tried to retrieve her slip.

'So many people here,' she answered evasively.

'But not you,' he said. 'You are different. So fresh, so unspoilt and your heart is free. Is not that a very wonderful and unique thing?'

'Yes, my heart is free,' Sheena said quickly. 'Pray do not let us speak of love. I find it a boring subject!'

'That is not true,' the Marquess said. 'No woman, if she is a true woman, which I am sure you are, could possibly be bored with love. But I will not speak of it in the way that I did before. That was a mistake, I know that now. Instead I will talk of myself, if you will allow me.'

'I doubt if I could stop you,' Sheena said with a little smile. 'But I think, my Lord Marquess, that I should be returning to the dancing.'

'Not yet,' he said. 'Please, not yet. Not until I have had time to tell you that I love you.'

'You love me!' she said in tones of utmost astonishment. 'What can you mean by that?'

'Exactly what I say,' he said. 'I love you. I love your little pointed face, your tiny, disdainful nose, the wonderment of youth in your eyes and, most of all, your mouth which was made for kisses.'

He bent towards her as he spoke and Sheena sprang to her feet.

'I think, my Lord, you make mock of me,' she said. 'Last time you told me that the King was in love with me, which was palpably untrue, and now you say that you, yourself, have a tenderness for me. Either you are deranged or making fun of me.'

'I am not crazed,' the Marquess said in a deep voice. 'I love you, Sheena. Give me a chance to prove my love. Listen to me sometimes. Let us find occasions in which to be together. For how can I ever convince you of my devotion or make you care for me if we never see each other?'

'I do not know what you mean by such a request,' Sheena said. 'We meet in the Court and we meet at other times.'

'You have got to believe me,' the Marquess said. 'I have to show you what love means—all that it means to a woman.'

'I am sorry, but I am not interested,' Sheena said.

'That is because you are so innocent,' the Marquess replied. 'Let me teach you a little about love.'

Before she suspected what he was about he had swept her into his arms. He held her very close and before she could struggle or cry out his lips were on hers. It was the first time in her whole life that she had been kissed and for a moment she was paralysed by the warmth and possessiveness of his mouth which held her prisoner.

And then in a sudden fury at his impertinence and her own submissiveness she fought against him, struggling to be free of his arms.

'How dare you?' she said as at last his lips no longer held her captive. 'How dare you? Let me go.'

'Sheena . . .' he pleaded, and then an icy voice from beside them said:

'Forgive me if I interrupt this very touching scene.'

As the Marquess's arms slackened, Sheena made a last effort and was free of him. Dishevelled and panting she turned round to see clearly in the moonlight the expression of cynical contempt on the Duc de Salvoire's face.

'Have you no tact?' she heard the Marquess ask angrily.

'I am but obeying orders,' the Duc replied, and the steel in his voice seemed to Sheena like a naked rapier. 'Your Queen has been asking for you, Mistress McCraggan.'

'Then I must go to her at once,' Sheena said.

'If you will permit me to accompany you I will show you where Her Majesty is waiting,' the Duc said formally.

He turned on his heel with only a look at the Marquess which would have annihilated a man less confident of his position, and then he and Sheena moved away side by side towards the entrance to the garden.

'I do not know what you must think of me,' Sheena said brokenly. 'I . . . I did not meet the Marquess by arrangement. I came away alone from . . . from the crowd . . .'

'There is no need to make any explanations to me, Mistress McCraggan,' the Duc said in his most bored, uncompromising voice, and her sentence died away and for some inexplicable reason she felt curiously near to tears.

How dared the Marquess behave in such a manner? she thought to herself, and then realised it was her own fault for having withdrawn from the crowd. Obviously in France a woman dared not be alone, for if a man were to find her unchaperoned she was instantly at the mercy of his desires.

Surreptitiously, as they walked on, she tidied her hair, conscious all the time that her mouth felt as if it was burning from the Marquess's kisses and her cheeks were flushed from the energy with which she had struggled against him.

They reached the end of the formal gardens and to her

surprise the Duc led the way towards the Palace. She would have questioned him but she felt she dare not submit herself any more to his sarcasm. She only thought miserably that he must think her a very abandoned and fast person because this was the second time he had found her trying to escape from the attentions of a strange man.

'How could I have helped it?' she wondered. And knew the answer was that she should not have wandered off alone.

The Duc opened a small garden door of the Palace and motioned her inside. They moved along a corridor and then to her surprise instead of going upstairs to the State Apartments he turned the handle of a door and stood aside to let her enter a small, book-lined room.

It was lit with a silver candelabra which revealed a great desk on the centre of which stood a pile of documents. There was a chair beside the desk and two others on either side of the hearth. Otherwise the room was barely furnished except for a huge portrait of the Duc himself which hung over the mantelpiece.

'This is my office,' the Duc said as if in answer to a question. 'Sit down, please.'

He indicated the chair in front of the desk and seating himself on the other side he opened a dispatch-box.

'But, the . . . the Queen . . .' Sheena stammered, as she obeyed the Duc almost automatically and sat down where he had indicated.

'Her Majesty asked for you, which is why I realised you were not present,' the Duc said. 'Before you go to her, I have something of importance to discuss with you.'

As he spoke he drew from the dispatch-box a number of letters. With a sudden leap of her heart Sheena recognised the writing on one.

'That is my letter,' she said accusingly. 'My letter to my father.'

'I know,' the Duc said. 'That is what I wish to discuss with you.'

'But . . . but why is it here?' Sheena asked. 'I was told . . .'

'You were told that it would be carried to Scotland in safety without surveillance,' the Duc said curtly. 'As it happens, the man you employed has been suspect for some time as being in the pay of Spain. When he left the Palace he went straight to the Spanish Ambassador who read all the letters that had been entrusted to the messenger before resealing them and telling the man to proceed on his way.'

'In the . . . pay of Spain!' Sheena said faintly. 'Then . . . then . . .'

'Then he is an enemy,' the Duc said. 'For, as you know, although technically we have signed a peace with Spain, she still remains the enemy of France and most surely the enemy of Scotland.'

'I did not know,' Sheena said.

'No, of course not,' the Duc replied. 'But in the meantime your letter has been brought to me and I think it only right to tell you that I have read it.'

'You have read it!' Sheena got to her feet. 'How dare you do such a thing? Surely it was bad enough that it should fall into the hands of our enemies without you prying into private correspondence without my permission.'

'Your permission was immaterial,' the Duc said. 'As the letters were carried by a spy, I had to know how deeply you were involved with him or with anyone else who might harm my country.'

'Is it likely that I should do anything of the sort?' Sheena asked.

'I am afraid it is possible to trust very few people these days,' the Duc said, 'as perhaps you, yourself, have found.'

It seemed to Sheena that there was a sneer in his words and she knew he was referring to the Marquess. She felt her cheeks flush.

'I have already tried to tell you,' she said, 'that I did not invite the Marquess to seek me out. Nor did I tolerate his behaviour save that I was too weak to fight as strongly against him as I shou'd have wished.'

'That I can understand,' the Duc said, but she fancied his lips curled.

Sheena stamped her foot.

'It is all very well to sit in judgment,' she said, 'but it is not easy for someone who comes from a quiet and decent land to understand the behaviour of the gentlemen at this Court.'

In answer the Duc picked up her letter.

'And yet I see you have a predilection for the Marquess,' he said. 'You describe him in most glowing terms to your father, while I am not so fortunate.'

'That letter was meant for my father's eyes and for no one else's,' Sheena said hotly. 'If I speak in glowing terms, as you describe it, of the Marquess, it was because I did not know him as well as I do now.'

'I hope that you now do know him well,' the Duc said, 'for you would, indeed, be wise to be warned against him. He is not the sort of companion that you should choose.'

'I do not think,' Sheena replied, 'that I have yet had the privilege of choosing any of my companions in the Palace. But I must, your Grace, reserve to myself the right to choose my own friends.'

She spoke hotly because he infuriated her, seated there, she thought, like a schoolmaster taking her to task, yet at the same time admitting that he had read a private letter which had never been intended for anyone's eyes save her father's.

She remembered uncomfortably the things she had written about him and as if the Duc knew what she was thinking he said with a twist of his lips:

'I see that I am not to be accorded the privilege of being one of those friends that you would choose.'

'You have certainly never attempted to show me any friendship,' Sheena retorted angrily.

She knew that in some ways she was in the wrong and it made her all the angrier. Her Scottish pride and her quick temper was blazing in her little face as she faced the Duc across the desk.

To her surprise he threw her letter down on the table and rose to his feet.

'Perhaps that is true,' he said. 'Perhaps I have not shown you the friendship I should have done. But I have lost the art of making friends. I have only become, as you so ably put it, utterly ruthless as an enemy.'

He walked across the room and back again while she stared at him in perplexity. She wanted to go on fighting him, but somehow he was no longer angry, only philoso-phising as he said in what was no longer a cynical voice but a tired one:

'How could one ever begin to explain Court life to a child from another world?'

'I am not a child,' Sheena answered.

He smiled at that and suddenly his expression was young and surprisingly tender.

'How young one must be to want to be old,' he said. 'I can remember saying the same thing myself when I was about your age and being furious because everyone laughed at me.'

Moving round the desk he stood beside Sheena and looked down at her.

'Let us forget what has happened,' he said, 'and start again. Will you allow me to say perhaps two things to you which it is necessary you shou'd know?'

'What are they?' Sheena asked suspiciously.

She was uncomfortably aware of her letter lying on the desk where he had thrown it, and remembered what she had written about the Queen as well as her remarks about the Marquess and the Duc.

'There is an old proverb,' the Duc said, ' "Beware of the Greeks when they come bearing gifts". And for the "Greeks" substitute "crowned heads".'

'Do you mean,' Sheena asked, puzzled, 'that . . .'

She hesitated a moment, remembering who had given

her gifts. Surely he could not mean the Queen. She looked up into his face.

'Beware of the Queen,' she said quietly. 'Is that what you are trying to say to me?'

'You must read your own interpretation into my remarks,' he said lightly, and turned away from her. 'But let me add something else. Have nothing to do with the Marquess de Maupré. Do not listen to him. Avoid him whenever you can.'

Because she did not understand all he was implying, and because in some inexplicable way she was frightened, Sheena said sharply:

'What do you mean by that? Why should you attack the Marquess?'

'Has he told you he is in love with you?' the Duc asked in a sneering voice. 'I can see from your face that he has. Well, do not believe him. He is in love with no one but himself and his whole heart and soul are engaged in prompting his own ambitions—the ambitions of a very ambitious man!'

More because the tone of contempt in his voice annoyed her than for any other reason Sheena was prepared to argue with him.

'Even the Marquess might be sincere sometimes,' she said.

'Do not be a little fool,' the Duc said testily. 'He is not in love with you and he never will be.'

Once again Sheena found it intolerable that he should speak to her in such a manner. 'How dare you address me like that?' she stormed. 'Why should I trust your judgment any more than that of the Marquess? You speak as if you have my well-being at heart, but one thing is very certain—you have no heart, no kindness for anyone or anything.'

She did not look at him as she spoke, she dared not. She drew in her breath quickly and continued:

'For some obscure reason you wish to take me to task. You insulted me before you saw me; you have sneered at and jibed at my country and everything that I, personally, have done since I came here. You read my private letters to my father and then talk as if you have the right to sit in judgment upon other people. I think you are despicable, utterly and completely despicable, and I will not listen to you.'

As if her words had pierced the Duc's guard he, too, flushed with anger.

'You little idiot,' he said. 'You are deliberately mis-understanding all I am trying to say to you. Think what you like about me, but beware how you trust the Marquess de Maupré. He is not to be trusted. The position he has adopted for himself at Court makes most decent people suspect and shun him. But you cannot be expected to understand that, so all I am doing is warning you to keep away from him. He will do you no good but only untold harm.'

'And why should I listen to you? How do I know that you are not telling me a pack of lies?' Sheena enquired.

'Because I know what I am talking about and you know nothing—not even how to keep yourself out of danger,' the Duc retorted.

'All I can reply is that I am tired of your insults,' Sheena said. 'I shall go to the Marquess now and tell him what you have said about him. I shall ask him to be my friend, to protect me from the intrigues and insults of people like you.'

Her voice was fiery with anger as she defied him and she fe't herself almost scorched by the fury in the Duc's eyes as he stared down at her.

'You will do nothing of the sort,' he shouted.

'I shall do what I wish without any interference from you,' Sheena retorted.

As if his self-control snapped, he bent forward suddenly and put a hand on each of her shoulders and shook her as one would shake a child who was being naughty.

'Listen to me, you little fool,' he said through clenched teeth. 'If you think you can play with fire in this place without getting burnt you are much mistaken. If you repeat one word of what I have said to you the consequence might be lamentable, not for me but for you. You are in danger, I tell you, and if you will not heed me then God knows what the outcome might be.'

'Let me go,' Sheena said breathlessly, as she tried to shake herself free of his strong hands which were hurting her shoulders.

'I will shake some sense into you,' he said, 'if it is the last thing I do.'

With a sudden movement she wrenched herself free of him.

'You are uncontrolled, unprincipled and a disgrace to your rank!' she stormed. 'I hate you! Do you hear me? I hate you!'

'Of course you hate me,' he said, equally angry. 'You only like those who suck up to you with sweet words, determined to use you for their own ends. Cannot you see, you conceited little Scot, that everything they say is insincere? Every word they utter is spoken with some ulterior motive.'

'I will not listen to you,' Sheena said. 'I am going now to find the Marquess and tell him just what you said about him.'

She made a movement to turn away, but the Duc reached out and caught her wrist with his hand.

'Very well then, go,' he said. 'I suppose it is his kisses you want. All women are the same. All they want from a man is love-making and more love-making. It is all they think about. They have no sense, no pride, no integrity— only an insatiable desire for what they call love.'

'Think what you like,' Sheena said murderously, her eyes flashing as she strove to free her wrist from his grip.

'Go and give him your lips and your heart and your trust,' the Duc said in his most cynical voice, 'and you will soon find out where you will end up and what harm it will do.'

'Let me go!' Sheena said, trying once more to pull herself free of him.

'Go to the Marquess,' the Duc said savagely, 'but if it is only kisses that you want—cheap, easy kisses which anyone can have for the asking—then why be content with his? Try mine! You may find them even sweeter.'

Before she could breathe, before she could take in what was happening, he had freed her wrist and pulled her roughly towards him. He cupped her chin with his fingers and threw her head back against his shoulder.

For a moment he looked into her eyes and she saw a strange, inner, uncontrollable passion in his. Then his mouth was on hers and he kissed her almost brutally with lips which seemed to take possession of her will so that she was powerless to move or even to struggle with him.

She felt his mouth holding her, felt for a moment as if she was diving down into the dark, mysterious depths of an ocean from which there was no return. She felt herself falling, felt something strange and utterly unreal happening to her.

And then as suddenly as he had seized her she was free. She staggered and would have fallen if she had not clutched at the chair to save herself.

'Go to the Marquess and be damned to you!'

He spoke in a low voice that was very different from the furious tones in which he had addressed her previously.

Then he walked away past the desk to the window on the other side of the room and pulled back the curtains with a jerky movement as if he sought the air. For a moment Sheena could only stare at him—at his square shoulders etched against the window. And then, without speaking and strangely without haste, she went from the room almost as if she were in a dream.

Sheena passed an unhappy, restless night. She tried to shut her mind to her thoughts and to the thumping of her heart, but after a while she realised that sleep was impossible and that her violent hatred of the Duc precluded all else.

As the dawn broke, pale and golden, and the first rays of light shone through the sides of the heavy curtains covering her window, she rose from her bed and walked across the room. She drew back the curtains and stood taking in deep breaths of the warm air, wishing that instead she was being buffeted by the sharp, strong winds blowing across the North Sea.

That was what she needed, she thought—the stimulating austerity and positiveness of Scotland. France made her feel weak and at the mercy of emotions she had never experienced before.

Always until now her beliefs had been unchallenged. Things were black or white, right or wrong, and she had no doubts, no uncertainties, either where her conscience was concerned or as to her line of conduct.

'Ye're either for the Lord or against Him.'

She could hear the minister thundering the words in the small, grey kirk she attended regularly at her father's side.

And now everything was so confused. Who was right and who was wrong? And where did she stand in it all? She could feel again the arms of the Marquess drawing her to him and his mouth fastening on hers. She felt again the inner revulsion, the shrinking and the dislike which made her struggle against him.

And then she could see the Duc's face, his eyes aflame with anger as he shook her before he held her close and yet closer.

Sheena opened wider the diamond-paned casements. She could not breathe—the air, her memories, her emotions were suffocating her. She felt as if the great Palace was closing in on her.

'I must get away,' she thought. 'I must get out into the countryside.'

She threw a wrapper around her shoulders and opening her bedroom door summoned one of the pages who was always in attendance in the corridors both day and night.

'I wish to go riding,' she said.

'Your pardon, Ma'mselle,' the page replied, 'but I have a message for you.'

'A message?' Sheena queried.

The page nodded.

'*Oui, Ma'mselle.* Her Majesty the Queen of Scotland wishes you to ride with her at half past eight. I was to have told you last night, but you had already retired.'

'Where am I to meet her?' Sheena asked.

'Her Majesty has ordered the horses to be at the South Gate,' the page replied.

Sheena nodded and went back into her room. She was used to receiving messages which were almost commands in such a manner. Mary Stuart would often determine at midnight some escapade or outing for the following day and messages were sent by the pages to those she wished to be in attendance on her.

Riding, Sheena knew, had become a new enthusiasm simply because Mary Stuart wished to emulate anything that the Duchesse de Valentinois did. The young Queen had almost a hero-worship for the older woman, and because of her attachment she had ordered her ladies-in-waiting to wear for their equestrian sport white with a touch of black in admiration of the Duchesse's famous fashion.

Sheena found herself, therefore, the possessor of a beautifully cut riding-habit of white velvet with a collar of black velvet trimmed with jet buttons. The first time she had worn it Mary Stuart exclaimed:

'You look enchanting, Sheena!' in her soft, seductive

112

tones. 'It makes your skin look like mother-of-pearl and your hair like a sunset over the Louvre.'

Sheena had blushed at the unaccustomed compliment and Mary Stuart laughed and putting her arm round her shoulders drew her face close to her own. Then she turned so that they both saw their reflection in the huge gilt mirror.

'Look,' she said. 'Was there ever anything more un-expected at a Court of dark, sloe-eyed women than three redheads? The Duchesse, you and me.'

Sheena thought at that moment that no one could hold a candle to the young Queen when she laughed and her face was animated. And yet in some extraordinary way both of them paled almost into insignificance beside the beauty of the Duchesse.

'Redheads!' Mary Stuart repeated, delighted at the phrase. 'The artists and the painters talk of our hair being Titian, Venetian, or Sienna tinged with gold, but you and I know that we have just a tangle of Scottish red and if we were living anywhere else in the world the boys would be calling us "carrots".'

When Mary Stuart was in this mood Sheena could not help adoring her.

'Are we not fortunate?' the Queen went on in her con-fiding manner which could make any man or woman her friend within a few seconds. 'It wou'd be terrible if we had any more rivals. Think how ordinary I shall look when I get to Scotland where every other woman has red hair.'

'You would never be anything but lovely and outstand-ing wherever you went,' Sheena said loyally.

'All the same, I like being unique,' Mary Stuart coun-tered. 'Do you know how I heard one of the courtiers describe me yesterday?'

'No, what did he say?' Sheena questioned.

'He said,' Mary Stuart answered, 'that I was like a statue of snow with a fire inside which would one day con-sume me.'

'What an unkind thing to say,' Sheena said hotly.

'No, no,' Mary Stuart replied. 'I liked that. I want to

think that I have a fire in my heart; that I shall be consumed by enjoying my life, by living it fully. I want to live, Sheena. I want to come alive and, above all, I want to love.'

Mary Stuart dropped her voice on the last word. There was a little tremor in it which told Sheena much more than her words. She put out her hand to take the little Queen's.

'You are young. There is so much time for all that later on,' she said. 'Be happy now with your friends. Soon there may be far more serious things to do.'

She was thinking as she spoke of the war against England, but Mary Stuart with a light laugh turned away from the mirror.

'There are, indeed, serious things in the future,' she said, 'for I am to be married. I shall be the Dauphine of France and, who knows?, perhaps sooner than anyone expects I might be Queen.'

'You are already a Queen,' Sheena reminded her.

'But who would not prefer to be Queen of two countries?' Mary Stuart said. 'And, better still, of three. A Triple Crown! Shall I ever wear it? I wonder.'

She was serious for a moment and then her eyes lit up.

'We will go and ask Nostrademus,' she said. 'Did you know that the Queen has invited him to come to Paris?'

'Who is Nostrademus?' Sheena asked.

'*Tiens!*' Mary Stuart exclaimed. 'Can you indeed be so ignorant? He is the greatest soothsayer in the whole world. His predictions are fabulous.'

'The Queen has asked him here?' Sheena asked.

'But, of course,' Mary Stuart replied. 'I have told you that the Queen is crazed on fortune-te'lers. She has even built a tower for them at the far end of the Palace near her apartments. The Ruggieir brothers work there, but they are old and dull and spend months making plans of the stars and the planets. There are other soothsayers too. The Queen does not really like our consulting them; she likes to keep them all for herself.'

'Surely she does not really believe them?' Sheena asked.

'Believe them!' Mary Stuart exclaimed. 'Her whole life centres round them. She follows all they say. She consults them a dozen times a day. And 'tis said . . .' Mary Stuart paused a moment and glanced over her shoulder as if to be sure that no one was within hearing, '. . . 'tis said that she attends secret rites of black magic.'

'What rubbish!' Sheena spoke scornfully. 'This Palace is full of such rumours. I have been told a dozen times that the Duchesse is a witch and that she has sold her soul to the devil so that she can remain young. But who really believes such foolishness?'

'The Queen for one,' Mary Stuart replied with a little twist of her lips; and then, as if bored with the conversation, she had turned eagerly towards a number of young people who had come into the room and prevented Sheena from saying more.

'They are all a bit touched in the brain,' Sheena thought to herself scornfully, knowing that such nonsense would never have been tolerated in Scotland.

At home there were people who were fey, who had the second sight, but witches and sorcerers and magicians were something to be credited only by the stupid superstitious English. They even believed that the Scotsmen carried magic claymores which could cleave a man's body in two without the owner exerting any strength whatsoever.

'Let them think such nonsense!' Sheena had heard her father exclaim more than once. 'A man is usually a coward when he believes he is up against the powers of evil.'

Yet as she dressed in her white velvet habit Sheena cou'd not help wondering if, in fact, the magic attributed to the Duchesse was such nonsense as one might suppose. It was incredible that she could be getting on for sixty, and yet look so young. There was not a line on her lovely face and her body was as slim and graceful as that of any young girl at Court.

Could there be something in the potions she was supposed to drink before she went out riding or the water in which she washed herself, not once but two and sometimes three times a day? Perhaps the answer lay in the salads and fruits she preferred to eat instead of the meat and venison and rich *pâtés* which everyone else consumed?

Maggie had told Sheena that the Queen's attendants swore that they had seen the devil with his cloven hoofs and tails gal'oping behind her on her morning ride; and Sheena had never been able to forget the tone of voice in which the men in the courtyard had denounced her for seducing and bewitching the King.

' 'Tis nonsense!' she said aloud. 'All nonsense!' And yet she could not help a shiver running through her body as, dressed in her white velvet habit, she waited for the hours to pass until it should be eight-thirty.

When a distant clock chimed the quarter-hour she set on her red hair a little tricorn black velvet hat trimmed with a sweeping white ostrich feather which curled down to her shoulder. She smiled at her reflection in the mirror before, picking up her embroidered gloves—a present from the Queen—and a riding-whip with a jewelled handle which Mary Stuart had lent her, she went from the room and started the long walk down the corridors to the door which led to the South Gate.

There were few people about at this time, for the Palace slept late. There were pages and chambermaids in the passages and an occasional glimpse of a gallant stumbling with a drunken gait and yawning mouth towards his own apartments. He would have spent the night gambling at cards or in the debauchery which made the younger set in the Palace the subject of unceasing gossip and condemnation.

Sheena, however, was too intent on her own thoughts to take much note of her surroundings. There were faint lines under her eyes this morning and her little mouth drooped a trifle wistfully. She looked lovely, but it was as if a film lay over her face hiding some of its youth and radiance.

She glanced out of one window as she passed and saw the garden through which she had walked the night before

116

with the Duc when he had brought her back to the house.

'I hate him!' she whispered beneath her breath, and felt the blood suddenly come coursing into her cheeks and her hands clench with the force of her emotions.

'I hate him! I hate him!'

The words seemed to repeat themselves over and over again as she walked down the polished stairs, her hand resting on the gilt and crystal banister.

She reached the doorway and saw that outside the horses were waiting. Eight perfect examples of highly bred horse-flesh champed at their silver bits and fidgeted restlessly as their grooms tried to calm them.

Mary Stuart's mount was ebony black with an embroidered saddle on which were emblazoned the arms of Scotland. At least, Sheena thought suddenly, they need not feel that her position as Queen was ever forgotten. Everywhere that it was possible for them to be painted, embroidered or portrayed, the arms of Scotland were to be found—in the young Queen's apartments, on her carriages or her servants' livery, and on her saddles.

The Queen of Scotland! And yet Sheena could not help asking her heart how much it really meant to Mary Stuart.

She heard a footstep behind her and saw one of the aides-de-camp come hurrying through the hall. He looked surprised when he saw Sheena.

'You did not receive my message, Mistress McCraggan?' he asked.

'Your message, Monsieur?' Sheena questioned, dropping him a small curtsy.

'Her Majesty has decided not to ride this morning. I sent pages to everyone's apartments, but yours must, alas, have arrived after you had left.'

'Her Majesty is not well?' Sheena asked in concern.

The equerry smiled.

'Her Majesty was very late last night,' he answered. 'When the dancing finished we all went boating on the lake and I am afraid one or two of the party were forced to swim for the shore.'

It was the sort of high-spirited horseplay which Mary Stuart would most enjoy, Sheena thought. At the same time she was glad she had not been there.

'We all got to bed when the sun was already above the horizon,' the aide-de-camp went on. 'I am sorry, Mistress McCraggan, that you should have risen early to no purpose.'

'On the contrary,' Sheena said. 'As I am ready, I shall ride.'

'I regret I cannot accompany you,' the aide-de-camp sighed.

'I do not want to sound rude,' Sheena answered, 'but I would rather be alone.'

She beckoned one of the grooms and he brought a horse to the mounting block. It was a beautiful animal, almost snow-white in colour, with embroidered reins and saddle cover of deep crimson velvet.

He assisted Sheena to mount, and she swung into the saddle feeling, as she had felt when she first awoke, a wild desire to be away from the Palace and out into the open air. She turned her horse's head towards the gate and knew that one of the grooms was following as she heard the clattering of his horse's hoofs on the cobbles behind her.

She did not look round or speak and the groom kept his distance, which gave her a sense of feeling free, of riding as if she were in Scotland, alone and unaccompanied with only the wind to talk to and the birds for companions.

It did not take long to be away from the streets and out into the open country. Here the King's great park rolled away to a distant horizon and the rides through the woods were empty save for a startled deer or a covey of partridges winging their way towards the open fields.

Sheena urged her horse faster. She wanted to get away from the Palace and from her own thoughts, and somehow only speed could achieve that. She brought her whip down lightly on the horse's flank and he sprang forward.

Faster, faster, she urged him on and then heard a sudden

cry from behind her. She looked back over her shoulder without slackening speed. The groom had dismounted and was raising his horse's hoof as if there was something wrong. A cast shoe or perhaps a stone lodged so that the animal had gone lame, Sheena thought.

The man shouted again, waving his cap, and Sheena turned her head and urged her own horse forward even faster. Nothing should stop her now. The groom could go home and relate what story he liked. All she knew was that she wanted to escape from the emotions and dreams of the night before, from the feel of the Marquess's arms around her and the touch of the Duc's lips on hers.

Faster! Faster! Would she ever forget the look in his eyes or the hard, angry possessiveness of his mouth? Her own was still bruised and once again she repeated the words which had been in her mind all the morning:

'I hate him!'

How long she rode she did not know. She only knew that at last her horse was tiring, and instinctively, because she loved animals, she drew in her rein and let him slow down, first to a trot and then to a walk.

They were both exhausted for the moment, and Sheena felt her own breath coming quickly between her parted lips. Yet somehow she already felt fresher and much more calm. The wood was thick and as the broad ride down which she had been galloping ended, she turned on to a narrow grass path leading between high pine trees.

Here at last she was at peace. How seldom, Sheena thought, was she ever alone! Always in the Palace there was someone chattering or talking, laughing or singing, as if all were afraid of their own thoughts and dared not be separated from the others.

And in her own bedchamber there was always Maggie— talking and gossiping, relating scraps of information she had acquired below stairs or else scolding or admonishing her for not doing what she thought was right.

Sheena drew a deep breath of relief. The groom was left behind. There was only herself and her horse and the soft sunshine percolating through the dark branches of the trees.

'Shall we run away and never come back?' she asked with a sudden whimsy, and she saw that the animal put back his ears as if trying to understand what she was saying.

She bent forward to pat him, and now the path was twisting a little to the right and to the left. The woods seemed to get thicker.

'Where are we going, do you think?' Sheena asked. 'And does it matter? Lead the way and perhaps we will find a new land with new people and escape from all the problems that are troubling us.'

She laughed a little at the sound of her own voice. How ridiculous she was being, she thought, talking to a horse! As if a horse cou'd have any problems except that of returning to its comfortable stable and enjoying a good meal of oats and hay.

She bent forward to pat his neck again and then raising her head realised almost with a sense of dismay that the wood was getting denser still. They had been moving for some time since they left the broad ride and she wondered where they could be and if it was possible to get lost.

'Supposing,' she said aloud, 'we wandered for hours and hours and never found our way home? You would be hungry and I should be frightened. I wonder if it is possible ever to be completely lost when we are so near to Paris?'

As if in answer to her question, she suddenly heard sounds a little ahead—the sounds of voices.

'We are not lost, after all,' she said with a little smile. 'Shall we retrace our steps or shall we enquire if there is a different way of returning? The latter would be more interesting.'

Answering her own question, she urged her horse forward and came suddenly through the wood and into a clearing. There was a house at one end of it which she guessed belonged to a woodcutter or someone of that sort, and to her surprise in the clearing and in front of the house there was a large crowd of people.

There must have been two or three dozen of them; all men, all apparently listening to one of their number who was standing on a fallen tree and addressing them.

Sheena came out from the darkness of the trees into the sunlight, and suddenly the speaker stopped his discourse and stared at her with open mouth. As his astonishment communicated itself wordlessly to the others the men all turned and they, too, stared wide-eyed as Sheena advanced slowly towards them.

They were all peasants, she noted, rough and unkempt and many of them with uncut beards. She thought the man who had been speaking to the others might be a preacher. But they all, for the moment, seemed paralysed by her appearance.

She could not understand why her arrival should astonish them so much; and yet as they stared and stared, their eyes broadening and their jaws dropping, she moved on towards them until her horse carried her within a few feet of the man still standing on the tree.

'Excuse me, Monsieur,' she said politely, 'but would you direct me back to Paris? I appear to have lost my way.'

As she finished speaking the man standing on the trunk of the tree gave a sudden shout.

' 'Tis she! 'Tis she!' he yelled in a strange, rather guttural dialect which Sheena had a little trouble in understanding. 'She has been sent to us. The Lord has delivered her into our hands.'

The men, as if at a word of command, all scrambled to their feet and surged round her. Sheena realised that they were putting out their hands to touch her horse and then the skirt of her riding-habit as if to reassure themselves that she was real and not a figment of their imagination.

' 'Tis she!' the preacher cried again. 'She has come to us.'

Sheena decided that he was a little mad.

121

'Pardon me,' she said again, 'but I am anxious to return to the Palace. Will one of you please show me the way?'

Without replying they all began to talk at once. Their voices were high and excited and Sheena found it very hard to understand their words. Over and over again it seemed to her they kept saying: 'She has come! She has been sent!'

And then suddenly it seemed to her that she sensed rather than felt there was something wrong. She pulled at her horse's bridle.

'I will go back the way I came,' she thought, and then realised with a sudden sense of dismay that she could not move. The men's hands were at the horse's head. They hemmed her in. They were shouting and arguing with one another and all the time they were looking at her and with a shudder she knew their eyes were full of hate.

'Let the horse go,' she said, at first quietly and then angrily: 'Let him go, I say.'

As no one heeded her it was obviously impossible for the horse to move. She bent forward with her whip, intending to tap lightly on the hands of those who held the reins, but the man who had been preaching from the tree-trunk sprang forward and before she realised what he was about seized the whip from her and taking it in his hands he broke it across his knee.

'That is what we must do to her!' he yelled. 'Break her as she has tried to break France. We can save our King; save him from the sorcery of this evil woman.'

It was both his words and the expression on his face which to'd Sheena what he thought.

'Listen,' she said, shouting above the noise. 'If you think I am the Duchesse de Valentinois you are mistaken. I am not the Duchesse.'

There was a sudden roar at the words and then Sheena found herself being dragged from the saddle, rough hands pulled her down and she felt herself thrust forward, half

122

carried, half propelled, until she stood beside the fallen tree-trunk, two men holding her hands behind her.

She was frightened, but she would not let them see it.

'Will you listen?' she said to the man who had been speaking when she arrived. 'I am not the Duchesse. I am Sheena McCraggan from Scotland. You have no right to treat me in this way.'

Even as she spoke she realised with horror that they were all past listening to her. Their leader was already on the fallen trunk again, haranguing the others, his voice, harsh and excitable, ringing out.

'The whore has been delivered into our hands!' he screamed. 'The harlot who has bewitched and enslaved our King is our prisoner. Here is the woman who by her evil magic has traduced our fair land and sold her own soul to the devil. What shall we do with her? Is it not right that we should punish her?'

'Yes! Yes!' the men roared back at him.

'We could make her suffer for her sins,' the speaker went on. 'We could flog her and humiliate her as our own people have been flogged and humiliated at her command. Or we could treat her as she has treated our friends and comrades—our comrades in the struggle for freedom. What has she done to them? I ask you, brothers, what has she done to them?'

There was a yell which seemed to blast its way into Sheena's ears.

'She has burnt them!' they roared.

'Then let us treat her likewise,' the preacher shouted. 'Let her feel the torment that she has meted out to others and let us pray that as she burns our King will be free of her and her spell will be destroyed.'

'Burn her! Burn her!' they yelled in unison.

With a sudden, unexpected movement Sheena wrenched herself free of the men who were holding her and reaching up caught the arm of the man standing above her on the tree-trunk.

'Look at me, you fool,' she said. 'I am young. I am only

seventeen. Can it be possible that you believe me to be the Duchesse who is an old woman?'

He looked down at her.

'The devil has made you fair,' he replied. 'See if the devil can save you now.'

She saw with a horror that was indescribable that his eyes were wild, the eyes of a fanatic, of a man driven beyond himself. She saw, too, that his oratory had brought a dribble of saliva to his lips and that he was almost in a state of ecstasy.

He shook his arm free of her and raised his hands towards the crowd.

'You have decided what is right and good,' he said. 'The Lord has been kind to us. But hurry, brothers, lest the devil who befriends her should spirit her away.'

With a terror that was almost intolerable, Sheena felt the rough hands holding her again and knew it would be impossible to escape. Each man's hold was like an iron clamp upon her delicate arm. At the same time she realised that they held her away from them as if the very nearness of her was a contamination.

They touched her, but they were afraid and she knew with a kind of sick help'essness that nothing she could say would convince them that she was not, in fact, the Duchesse de Valentinois.

And now the preacher on the tree-trunk had burst into wild prayer—a prayer of thankfulness to God for delivering the King's harlot into their hands and for giving them the opportunity to rid France of the scourge that had lain on all of them these past ten years.

'Send her, O Lord,' he was shouting, 'into the hell of the damned. Let her unclean body burn and rot until the worms destroy it. Let her heart be eaten by the dogs and her eyes be gouged out by the birds of prey.'

It could not be true! This could not be happening to her, Sheena thought. She, too, wanted to pray, and yet no words would come to her. She could only stand captive, and yet, at the same time, conscious of a kind of strange numbness which made it impossible for her to cry or even to ask again for mercy.

She watched the men come running from the wood with a high stake which they placed in the middle of the clearing. One man climbed upon another's shoulders and hammered it into position. And others came bearing sticks, logs and branches of trees which they grouped around the stake until the pile was about three feet off the ground.

At last Sheena realised that they were ready and they turned, as if awaiting further instructions, to the man who was still praying, the froth from his mouth running down over his chin and beard.

She remembered then how the men like him had shrieked at the Duchesse as she and the King had walked up the steps of the Palace and how Mary Stuart had told her that they would be burnt at the stake. She knew now, although she had never heard what had happened to them, that that had been done.

There was no hope for her, no reprieve, and she could only pray, with some faraway, critical part of herself, that her pride would sustain her and that she would not die ignominiously and as was unbefitting to a Scot.

At the same time she was practical enough to know that there was no point in pleading, that nothing she could say would either be listened to or heard. These men had faith in their cause, believed what they were saying was the truth. And she was not dealing with ordinary people.

The stake was finished and the last man to throw a log at the foot of it came towards her. He was a big, burly man, and by his bulging muscles and the leather apron he wore Sheena guessed that he was a blacksmith. He shouted at the preacher, interrupting his prayers.

'Is the devil's spawn ready for the burning?'

The man who was praying stopped abruptly.

'She is ready,' he replied. 'And be careful that she's tied tightly to the stake and that Satan himself cannot come on wings and carry her off.'

The blacksmith hesitated a moment.

'Will she burn as she is?' he asked. 'Or like our own people, with little to cover them save a shift?'

'Do we treat a harlot any better than those who have found favour with the Lord?' the preacher enquired.

Sheena then tried to struggle, but there was nothing she could do. The blacksmith put out his great hand and pulled at the jacket of her velvet habit. The jet buttons burst and scattered on the ground and he dragged it from her shoulders and off her arms, and although she tried to clutch at her skirt it, too, was torn from her.

Then she had to cease struggling and try to hold the torn remnants of her shift across her naked breasts. The blacksmith picked her up in his arms and carried her to the stake. She smelt the pungent, animal smell of him and the smell, too, of excitement and fear.

He set her down on top of the pile of logs and there were other hands as well as his binding her with ropes around the waist to below her knees.

She tried again to clutch at her shift and hold it across her breasts, but it was impossible and she stood there naked to the waist and she knew, in some manner which made it almost worse, that the men's eyes who beheld her were filled only with loathing and disgust.

She was tied securely. The ropes cut into her soft flesh and hurt her almost unbearably, but even as she thought of it she realised how stupid it was to complain when the pain she was to feel a few moments later would be so much worse.

She crossed her hands over her breasts and knew that she was trembling with fear and yet she was still in possession of enough self-control to try one more plea.

'I wish to speak,' she cried. 'Hear me! Hear me!'

The chatter of tongues ceased for one moment.

'I am innocent,' she told them. 'I am not the Duchesse de Valentinois. I come from Scotland. If you burn me you will burn only someone who has done you no harm. Believe me, for I speak the truth and in the name of God I beg of you to let me go.'

126

There was silence for a moment as she finished and then with a great shout the man who had been praying yelled:

' 'Tis a trick! She lies to save herself! 'Tis a trick! Close your ears, brothers, and do the will of God which is to free the world of such filth.'

Hurriedly, as if they were half ashamed of having listened, the men surged forward to do his bidding. One man had kindled a flame to a piece of wood and now the others ran towards him, thrusting other pieces into the darting fire and shielding them with their hands against the wind.

Sheena shut her eyes. She thought of Scotland and of the quiet and peace of the moors, of the burn at the end of the garden trickling down over the stones. She thought of her mother and felt somehow that she was near her.

'Make me brave,' she whispered. 'Let them not see how frightened I am. Please, God, do not let me scream at the pain.'

There was the smell of smoke in her nostrils and she opened her eyes to see the men already kind'ing the logs at the bottom of the pile. It would be some time before the fire reached her, and yet already the little flames were beginning to dart amongst the brushwood, running along a branch and then petering out, only to be revived again elsewhere.

The preacher was at his prayers again.

'We burn this woman, O Lord, as we burn away the sins of those who blacken the fair name of France. Destroy her and destroy all those who batter down the poor and hungry and exalt only the rich. Help us to throw off all that is corrupt and wicked in our midst and save our King that he may rule over us in decency and pureness of heart.'

Other voices joined in.

'Burn her, O Lord! Burn her! And let the evil she has perpetrated die with her.'

'Burn her! Burn her!'

The men repeated themselves over and over again. The flames were creeping higher. The smoke was beginning to overpower Sheena and she could feel her eyes smart and water.

The voice of the preacher was rising excitedly. Now he was almost in a frenzy.

'May all harlots, all whores, be destroyed in such a manner,' he was screaming. 'Bring down upon them the wrath and destruction of the Lord. May they rot in the hell of their own creating. May they burn as those who have died for right have burned, but in the torment not only of the mind but of the soul.'

Sheena felt a sudden flame flicker on her foot and bit back a scream of pain as it rose in her throat. Now it was coming. She was going to be burnt and her body would be charred black and lifeless and no one would ever know what had happened to her.

She wanted to cry out and yet still her pride kept her silent.

'Oh, God, save me!' she whispered, and she longed in that moment to have someone to call on for help. Her father—how far away he was! She had no friends, no one who would think of her when she was dead.

Almost unbidden, the Duc's face came to her mind and even as it did so she heard a sudden shout from the men around her. It was a shout not of exaltation but of fear.

'They are coming!'

She heard the words distinctly and then there was the clatter of harness and horses' hoofs, of men's voices and the scream of those who were injured. She saw someone on a horse gallop up to the preacher and run him through with a sword so that his body for one moment stood suspended on the log, his mouth open, his eyes protruding, before he toppled over backwards, blood gushing over his shirt.

There seemed to Sheena to be horses and men everywhere. The flame was licking again at her foot and she shut her eyes in an effort not to scream, then realised that there were men at her side kicking the burning logs away from the stake.

There were screams of terror and agony, the snorts of horses and the jangle of harnesses. The rope which bound her to the stake was being cut. She would have fallen if someone had not put his arms round her.

She knew who it was and still she dare not open her eyes. It was not only that she did not wish to look at him, it was because she was ashamed of her own nakedness, of her bare breasts smudged a little with smoke and her torn shift gathered over her hips.

Then as she stumbled forward a soft velvet cloak enveloped her and strong arms lifted her off the ground.

'Is she badly burned?' she heard someone ask and the Duc's voice above her head replied:

'I think not, but the shock must have been terrible, poor child.'

She had never heard such kindness in his voice before. Surprised more than anything else, she opened her eyes and looked up at him. His face was not very far from hers.

'It is all right,' he said quietly. 'You are safe.'

To her dismay her self-control broke and her whole body was racked with sobs. She hid her face against his shoulder and cried uncontrollably, as a child might cry who had been alone and frightened in the dark.

'It is all right, it is all right,' she heard him mutter. She felt him lift her on to the front of his saddle and spring up behind her. Then the noise and the shouting were left behind and they were riding quietly through the wood.

Gradually the tempest of her tears ceased and while she still hid her face against him and her breath came in quick sobs she was no longer shaken by a torrent she could not control.

'It is all right, Sheena,' she heard him say very quietly. 'You are safe now, thank God.'

She thought at that moment that she had never realised before how strong and comforting a man's arms could be.

9

Sheena lay on a couch with her eyes closed. She could feel some of the tension leaving her body and letting her breathe quietly and normally again. The physician had treated her burned feet and bandaged them, and now they were covered with a soft, silk rug which bore the arms of Scotland.

For the moment she could hardly remember all the terror and panic which had been hers when she thought that she was about to die. Yet it seemed to her now that never had life been so desirable, so wonderful, so exciting and with so much promise.

She remembered how once she had stood with her father watching a company of soldiers marching to battle and, as they passed, whistling gaily and waving to the crofters who had cheered them on their way, he had said:

'They give their lives gladly; they have nothing else to give.'

But looking at the sunshine glinting over the moors, the touch of snow on the tops of the mountains, and hearing the waves breaking on the shore, Sheena had thought how hard it must be to give up one's life: how desperately difficult to go willingly on a journey from which there is no return.

She knew that as she had stood bound at the stake, praying that her pride would hold and sustain her, she had longed passionately to live. And she was convinced now that life, however difficult and complex, however troub'esome and treacherous, was preferable in every way to surrendering oneself to the darkness and the uncertainty of death.

'I am alive!' She had repeated the words silently until suddenly she found that she had said them aloud, and she opened her eyes to see the Duchesse de Valentinois coming into her bedchamber.

For a moment Sheena stiffened, hating the Duchesse for what she had suffered on her account. Then she saw that there were tears in the Duchesse's beautiful eyes as she came towards the couch and bent down to take Sheena's hand in hers.

'How can I ever tell you, my child, what are my feelings that you should have suffffered in this manner on my account?' she said in her soft, low, musical voice.

'It is . . . nothing, Madame,' Sheena replied, feeling somewhat at a disadvantage as she lay looking up into the Duchesse's face.

'On the contrary, it is everything. It is wrong and shaming,' the Duchesse said. 'The King and I are both humiliated that a visitor from another land, a guest under the shelter of our roof, should have been treated in such a manner. If it had not been for the Duc de Salvoire, Heaven knows what might have happened.'

'The Duc?' Sheena questioned.

'Yes, indeed,' the Duchesse replied. 'It was he who saved you. Did you not know?'

'I . . . I knew that he came to my rescue as the . . . the flames were beginning to . . . burn my feet,' Sheena stammered. 'But I did not understand why.'

'The Duc was out riding with a number of his friends,' the Duchesse explained. 'He saw your groom leading a lame horse back towards the Palace and asked him what was amiss. The man told him that you had gone on ahead alone, that he had been unable to keep up with you.'

The Duchesse paused a moment and then went on, her voice warming:

'Anyone else might have thought it of little consequence, but the Duc sometimes has an instinct which has served him in war and has now served him to save your life. He felt—as the old peasants say—in his bones that something was wrong. He called to his friends who were moving off in another direction and gathered them together. He told them what none of us knew at the time, that he had heard rumours about a band of reformers who had a

131

secret hiding-place somewhere in the woods where they met and plotted against the true faith.'

'He knew they were there?' Sheena asked.

'Not actually,' the Duchesse replied. 'He had only been informed quite unofficially that one of the woodmen was not to be trusted. It was just a small piece of gossip such as echoes round the Palace day after day and to which usual'y nobody pays the slightest heed. The Duc remembered it.'

The Duchesse gave a little sigh and sat down on the edge of the couch, holding Sheena's hand in both of hers.

'I thank God from the bottom of my heart that he was in time,' she said. 'I have sent a gift to Notre-Dame and to the nunnery of Les Filles de Dieu, to express my gratitude that you were saved.'

She bent forward and with soft, gentle fingers soothed Sheena's hair back from her brow.

'What you must have suffered, my poor child,' she went on. 'It is impossible to realise the agony of your mind or your feelings when you were handled so roughly by those terrible men.'

'I am glad it was not you, Madame,' Sheena replied, and to her own surprise meant it.

'I doubt if I should have been as brave as you were,' the Duchesse answered. 'The Duc told me that when he found you you were not screaming or crying, but standing with your face raised towards the sky. How many of us would have the courage to face death in such a way?'

'Neverthe'ess I was afraid, Madame,' Sheena confessed. 'Desperately, horribly afraid. Those men, they were a little mad I think.'

'Very mad, both in their minds and in their souls,' the Duchesse replied.

She rose from the couch and walked towards the window and back again, twisting her hands together. Every movement that she made was one of beauty, and yet for the first time since she had first seen her Sheena saw the lines of trouble and worry on her face and the expression of one who is tortured by her thoughts.

'They meant to kill me,' she said softly, almost as if she was talking to herself. 'They meant to kill me—and perhaps it would have been better if they had.'

Sheena said nothing and after a moment the Duchesse went on still in that low voice:

'I cannot tell you how I have prayed that men like the Reformers should not be permitted to agitate and distress our gentle, peace-loving countrymen. And yet everywhere they go they stir up agitation.'

'What do they hope to gain?' Sheena asked.

'Do you realise that this is a movement which is happening all over Europe?' the Duchesse replied. 'You have such men in your own country and their leader, I understand, is called John Knox. Where there are many of them they call themselves the Reformers, although sometimes they are known as Protestants. But always they seek to turn people from the true faith, from the worship of God and their loyalty to the King.'

She gave a little sigh and then something which was half a laugh.

'I am their scapegoat!' she explained. 'If it were not me it would be someone else. But because I am in the position that I am it is easy to accuse me of every foul crime and bestiality that is known to mankind.'

She made a gesture of helplessness before she continued:

'But what they really require to be rid of is the Catholic faith, the faith of our fathers, the faith in which France has stood rooted since Christianity first brought a light into the world.'

'And what religion do they offer instead?' Sheena asked.

'That is just the point,' the Duchesse answered. 'If they offered something quite different, another God perhaps, a different Trinity, one could understand it. But they take faith from a man and give him nothing in exchange except a desire to destroy all that is stable, just and decent.'

She spoke with such feeling and Sheena could not help being a little moved even while deep in her heart she knew that the Duchesse, however good her intentions, was living a life of sin.

The Duchesse moved back to the couch and seated herself again.

'I am going to tell you something, little Sheena,' she said, 'that I have never told anyone else—not even the King. A few weeks ago when the Reformers reviled me, and said such things that any woman's heart must shrivel within her when she listened, I went to see the Cardinal de Guise. You know him?'

Sheena nodded her head. She had seen the Cardinal, tall, stately and very impressive in his red robes, at all the Court functions, and once as she genuflected to him in the passage he had held out his hand that she might kiss his ring in passing.

'I told the Cardinal,' the Duchesse went on, 'that I was deeply distressed at what was happening in France and I asked him if it was my duty to leave the world behind and to take the veil in a nunnery. "Direct me, your Grace," I begged him . . .'

The Duchesse's voice broke for a moment and Sheena, listening wide-eyed, saw that such an action must have come after long and difficult nights of prayer, wrestling with her conscience and her desire to serve France.

'What did the Cardinal say?' she asked, fascinated to such an extent by what the Duchesse was saying that she felt she must know the answer.

'He did not speak at first,' the Duchesse replied, 'and finally, when I could bear the silence no longer, I cried: "Which way can I best serve my God and France?" The Cardinal twisted his heavy jewelled ring. "The way of selflessness," he answered me. "The Duchesse de Valentinois has a higher mission than to leave the world, even in the service of God—a mission which no one but she could perform." '

'He told you to stay!' Sheena exclaimed.

The Duchesse bowed her head as if for a moment the burden she had undertaken was intolerable.

'Who else would guide the King?' she asked. 'Who else would show him the difficulties and the treacheries of statesmanship which his father would never let him learn? Who else could be strong enough to rid France of these men who threaten to undermine her very soul?'

The Duchesse jumped to her feet.

'Torture, death and the stake!' she cried. 'Could anything be more against the gentle teaching of our Lord Jesus? And yet what alternative is there? To let innocent people suffer? To let these anarchists—for they are little more—undermine the Monarchy and our country?'

The Duchesse clasped her hands together as if in prayer.

'They must be destroyed!' she whispered. 'They must! They must!'

There was so much passion and intensity in her tone that Sheena felt the tears start to her eyes, and then in a low voice she asked:

'The men who tried to kill me; what . . . what will happen to them?'

The Duchesse wheeled round to face her.

'Those who are left alive will die at the stake.'

'Oh, no! No, not that!' Sheena pleaded.

'It must be so,' the Duchesse said quietly. 'Not only because they tried to kill me and captured you by mistake but because they are fighting against the God in which we believe, the faith in which lies the only hope of salvation.'

Sheena shut her eyes for a moment. Somehow it seemed to her that the Duchesse was equally fanatic in her way as the preacher had been in his. Was there no other course? she wondered; something less extreme; something quiet, wiser and easy to live with.

Then she heard the Duchesse say quietly:

'You are tired. I have talked to you too much. Forgive me, but what has happened to you has been a shock to me, even though a lesser one than yours.'

She bent down and pressed her lips against Sheena's forehead. There was the soft, sweet scent of flowers, a touch on her hands from a white silk robe, then the

Duchesse had gone from the room, closing the door gently.

It seemed to Sheena that she left behind her innumerable questions and problems to which there was apparently no answer. And then, because she was desperately tired, she must have dozed a little, for she awoke with a start as the door opened and there were subdued giggles and laughter outside. She turned her head to see Mary Stuart accompanied by half a dozen of her friends come into the room, her arms filled with white carnations.

'Oh, you are awake!' she exclaimed with relief. 'Your maid threatened us with the most dire punishments if we awoke you. What a dragon she is and how I adore the Scots when they are fierce!'

She threw her armful of carnations on to the silk rug which covered Sheena's feet and then said:

'Oh, Sheena, we have been so worried about you. What a ghastly adventure! And yet, at the same time, how exciting—to be burnt at the stake and yet to survive! What a story you will have to tell for all time.'

''Tis one I would forgo with the greatest pleasure,' Sheena replied with a little smile.

'Tell us what it was like,' Mary Stuart begged. 'Were you terrified? Did your flesh creep and yet at the same time did you feel somehow elated because your soul was about to soar to Heaven?'

'I am afraid now I am not sure exactly what I did feel,' Sheena said apologetically.

'Oh, how disappointing you are,' Mary Stuart pouted. 'I have often wondered what it would be like to meet death—at the stake or at the block. I have even dreamed sometimes of walking towards the headsman, seeing his eyes behind the black mask glinting at me.'

A shudder went through Sheena and she put her hands up to her face.

'No, no!' she cried. 'Do not say such things.'

But Mary Stuart's companions laughed.

'Her Majesty is always imagining that she is the centre of some terrible drama,' one of her ladies-in-waiting

136

teased. 'She told me once exactly what one felt when one was drowned at sea.'

'There are many ways of dying,' Mary Stuart said, 'and Sheena has experienced one of them. She must tell us what it was like. She must!'

'Not now,' Sheena said quickly, knowing how insistent the little Queen could be when she wanted something. 'I must have time to collect my thoughts and put them into the proper words.'

'Then I will tell a story to make you all afraid of the dark. Perhaps I shall die that way,' Mary Stuart said, drawing the attention back to herself. 'I shall feel the flames leaping towards me, hear the crackling and know that in a few seconds my white flesh will turn black.'

A young Frenchwoman gave a little scream.

'Save us, Ma'am! Save us from such ideas. We are here to commiserate with Sheena, not to make her live that ghastly experience all over again!'

'I am sorry, it is tactless of me,' Mary Stuart apologised with her flashing smile. 'And to cheer you up, Sheena, we have a treat for you.'

'What is that?' Sheena asked.

'We have arranged for the Queen's latest fortune-teller to meet us here. Nostrademus himself has promised to come. What do you think of that?'

'I think it is a waste of a good afternoon when you might be doing something much more amusing,' Sheena answered.

Mary Stuart laughed.

'Is not that like Sheena?' she said. 'Always so practical; making out that we are feather-brained fools. Well, in this at any rate she shall not have her way. I am simply longing to hear Nostrademus.'

'And so am I,' the others chorused.

There came a knock at the door.

'There he is!' Mary Stuart exclaimed. 'Let him in quickly.'

Someone ran to obey and through the doorway came a

small, thin, middle-aged man with deep-set eyes, high cheek-bones and long, thin fingers with big joints. He carried a number of rolled-up parchments under his arm and Sheena noticed that his doublet was shabby and his hose had been constantly repaired.

Nostrademus bowed low. Mary Stuart gave him her hand to kiss.

'We heard of your fame, Monsieur,' she said. 'We heard that your prophecies invariably come true and that you see into the future more clearly than anyone else in the whole world.'

'Your Majesty flatters me,' Nostrademus replied, in a low, deep voice which seemed to come from the very depths of his body.

'Tell us our fortunes,' Mary Stuart begged. 'Tell us what you see for us.'

Nostrademus smiled.

'You are young,' he said, 'and the future is something which lies so far ahead that you are not afraid of it. But all too quickly it will become the present and then the past.'

'Tell me what you see for me,' Mary Stuart insisted. 'Will I wear the Triple Crown? Shall I be Queen of France, Scotland and England?'

Nostrademus seemed to look at her searchingly, then crossing the room he laid the parchments beneath his arm on the small escritoire which stood in front of the window.

'If your Majesty will permit me,' he said, indicating a chair.

'Of course, of course,' Mary Stuart agreed impatiently.

He spread out his charts in front of him.

'When were you born?' he asked.

It was the first of a large number of questions, all of which he wrote down very slowly with a long quill pen which squeaked a little on the parchment.

Finally he said:

'You are beautiful and men will always love you, but your beauty will not bring you happiness. Jealousy will

138

always be a bitter enemy and especially when it comes from one particular woman who wears a crown. There is marriage; you will be a widow and the wife of someone who is not worthy of you.'

He paused for a moment. There was silence in the room as everyone listened to him, wide-eyed. He looked down at his chart and then finally he said:

'There are hearts and swords, violence and tears, around you. You will wear a crown. You will love passionately and be loved with passion. Let that suffice.'

'No, no, tell me! Tell me all that you see!' Mary Stuart commanded imperiously.

Nostrademus turned over his chart.

'That is all,' he said quietly.

There was something in his face which made Sheena uneasily aware that he could say a great deal more if he wished.

'That is all,' he repeated.

'At least my life will be exciting,' Mary Stuart said with glittering eyes. 'At least I shall not be bored. Love! That is something with which a woman can never be bored. Is not that true, Monsieur?'

'Love comes in many different ways,' he answered, 'especially to a Queen.'

'A Queen is still a woman,' Mary Stuart said.

He began to gather up his papers.

'Wait!' she cried. 'You have not done my friends. And what about my fiancé, the Dauphin?'

'I regret, your Majesty, I can only do one person at a time,' he answered. 'You will understand that once I have concentrated on them their personality comes between me and anyone else. Another day perhaps.'

'Yes, yes, of course,' Mary Stuart replied. 'We will visit you tomorrow.'

It was obvious that having had her own fortune told she was not particularly concerned with anybody else's.

Nostrademus put his documents under his arm and turned towards the door. And then, as if for the first time, he saw Sheena lying on the couch, and almost as if he was compelled he walked towards her.

'Is it you, Ma'mselle, who met with such an unfortunate accident in the woods this morning?' he asked.

Sheena nodded.

'The Palace can talk of little else,' he said. 'May I express my sympathy for what you must have suffered?'

'Thank you,' Sheena said quietly.

He looked down at her and then he bowed low.

'Sometimes such a doleful experience to the body can bring delight to the heart,' he said.

Sheena looked up at him in a puzzled manner, and then before she could question him, or even quite understand what he had said, he had bowed and gone from the room.

Mary Stuart was still chattering about her future.

'Love and danger! Do the two things go together?' she questioned, and then laughed delightedly at some impudent sally from one of the young courtiers who was always in attendance on her.

Chattering and laughing like peacocks, the colourful little band withdrew from Sheena's room, going in search of other entertainment in another part of the Pa'ace.

The room seemed strangely quiet without them; and now, at last, Sheena was forced to fix her own thoughts, to remember what had happened and feel again the humiliation of the moment when they had torn her clothes from her and the horror of being carried in the blacksmith's arms towards the stake.

She was lost in remembering and did not hear the door open. It was therefore with almost a frightened start that she looked up and found the Duc standing beside her. For a moment she was angry that he should have entered so quietly that she had not heard him or, indeed, bade him come in. Then the memory of how he had seen her naked and covered her with his cloak brought a crimson flush to her white face and her eyes fell before his.

'You are better?' he asked.

'Y . . . yes, thank you.'

She found it difficult to say the words and prayed that he would go away quickly, for her voice seemed choked in her throat. Instead he fetched a chair and putting it beside her sat down in it.

'The physician tells me that your feet are not as bad as he first anticipated.'

'They do not hurt me now,' Sheena answered.

He sat looking at her and after a moment she forced herself to say:

'I . . . I must thank your Grace for . . . coming to my rescue.'

'There is nothing to thank me for,' he replied quietly.

'On the contrary,' she insisted. 'The Duchesse tells me that if it had not been for you I . . . I should not be here at this moment.'

'How could you have been so foolish as to leave your groom behind?'

Looking back, Sheena remembered why she had been so angry, why she had wanted to escape from the confines of the Palace and to ride wildly off into the woods until she and her horse were exhausted. Yet how could she tell him the reason? She coloured again.

As if he half guessed what she was feeling, he did not wait for her answer but went on:

'The King has given orders that in future no one will ride from the Palace except accompanied not only by a gentleman armed with a sword but also by two grooms. The next victim may not be so lucky.'

'But I understand that the men who . . . who captured me will be put to death,' Sheena said.

'Others will come and take their place,' the Duc answered. 'Sometimes I think that we are trying to push back an encroaching tide with no other weapons but bare hands.'

There was a cynicism in his voice which was very unlike the passionate fanaticism of the Duchesse.

'But you cannot believe these men to be right,' Sheena said.

'What is right and what is wrong?' the Duc asked.

141

'Have you not found that a puzzling question since you came to the Court of France?'

Sheena looked at him in surprise, astonished that he should have guessed so correctly her perplexities or have known how difficult she was finding it to form a clear and honest opinion of anything and anybody.

To her amazement the Duc bent forward and laid his hand on hers. At the touch of his strong fingers she was suddenly still; feeling as if she could not move, could not even breathe.

'Go away,' he said harshly. 'Go back to Scotland before you are spoilt and disillusioned. You came here so positive, so sure of yourself and your loyalty. If you stay here much longer you will be bewildered, unhappy and perhaps, who knows?, as cynical as I am myse'f.'

His lips curled derisively at the last words and then he rose to his feet.

'Go away, little Sheena,' he said. 'That is my advice to you. There are things here in the Palace that I cannot explain and which you are too young to understand. But if you take my advice you will follow your letter as quickly as possible.'

'My letter?' Sheena queried.

'I have sent it to your father,' he explained. 'It is assigned by someone sure and trustworthy. He will get it.'

'Thank you,' Sheena said, and then added quickly, lest she should find it hard to say: 'I have not thanked you properly. You have not let me tell you how grateful I am for coming when you did, for saving me . . . from . . . d . . . death.'

There was an expression on the Duc's face which she did not understand.

'Perhaps I heard you calling me,' he said unexpectedly; and then before she could recover from her bewilderment he had gone from the room.

She was so surprised that she turned her head to look at the door which had closed behind him. What did he mean by that? For, indeed, she had not called him. Not one word had passed her lips.

Deep in her heart something stirred. It was not really a memory but something less explicable, more obscure. It was a re-echo, perhaps, of something she had felt and which at the time had not been able to put into words. What was it? She could not explain it to herself.

Then quite suddenly, like a light coming through the window, she knew that all through the terror and horror and fear of what she had experienced she had known that she was not going to die. She had known unmistakably and yet absolutely that she would live and be saved.

And she had known, although until this moment she had not been sure of it, that the person who would save her would be the Duc.

10

Sheena walked quickly towards Mary Stuart's apartments, hurrying as if every moment was precious and she had no time to spare. She had been doing the same thing all day. Hurrying, bustling and pretending that she was too engaged even to have time to greet the courtiers she passed in the passages.

But in reality she was running away from herself, from her thoughts, from the feeling that sooner or later she had got to analyse her own emotions and discover the truth.

She reached the young Queen's apartments and found the ante-chamber empty and the door into the salon ajar. Through it she heard voices—Mary Stuart's, high, excited, musical, and another voice, a man's.

She paused, thinking perhaps she was intruding, wondering whether she should knock and enter or wait until whoever was engaged with the Queen came out.

'Do not be cross with me, your Eminence,' she heard

Mary Stuart say. 'You must not forget I am growing up.'

'I have not forgotten it,' came the quiet, deep voice of Cardinal de Guise. 'But growing up carries new responsibilities, new duties and new commitments.'

'I am not as old as all that.'

Sheena could almost see the little sidelong glance under her long eyelashes that Mary Stuart would give the Cardinal as she spoke.

He did not reply, and after a moment she went on:

'I am so happy here in France. Everyone is so kind to me, and now, as well as my fiancé, I have *beaux*, many *beaux*. Has your Eminence not noticed it?'

'I have indeed,' the Cardinal replied. 'It is right that your Majesty should be admired. But I should not be doing my duty as your confessor if I did not warn you that to play with men's hearts is also to play with fire.'

'And yet, like a fire, it is warming and exciting,' Mary Stuart answered. 'I like men, your Eminence. I like them around me. I like to talk to them. I like to see the admiration in their eyes and to know that I have power over them.'

'Your Majesty is very frank, but what you say gives me thought for deep anxiety,' the Cardinal replied. 'It is a woman's privilege to desire admiration, but like a strong liquor one must not drink too deeply from the cup but must sip it sparingly.'

'But I do not wish to be cautious, careful and old!' Mary Stuart exclaimed. 'Although I may be growing up, I still want to be young, I want to enjoy life, I want to savour every moment of it.'

There was a pause and Sheena guessed that the Cardinal was looking at the young Queen in perplexity. Then he said quietly:

'You have many fond and devoted women in your entourage. May I suggest that you cultivate their friendship and perhaps learn from them to be a little more . . . discreet, a little more careful on whom you bestow your affections?'

'Women are bores!'

There was a note of defiance in Mary Stuart's voice now and Sheena guessed that her red mouth was drooping a little as it was wont to do when anyone crossed her wishes.

'Not all women,' the Cardinal said with a touch of amusement in his voice. 'Surely you have a great deal in common with little Mistress McCraggan who has recently arrived from your own country?'

Mary Stuart gave a little laugh.

'Sheena is what your Eminence would call "a really nice girl",' she said. 'But as for having much in common, tell me where our interests can meet? She talks always of Scotland, a barren, cold, poverty-stricken land from all I have learned of it. I love France. I want to live here at Court. I want one day to be your Queen.'

Sheena put her fingers to her mouth to stifle a little ex-clamation of horror. What would her father and the Elders think, she wondered, if they could hear their Queen speaking in such a manner?

'And what of England?' she heard the Cardinal enquire.

'I wish too, of course, to be Queen of England,' Mary Stuart replied. 'A Triple Crown! It would be the first time in all history that a woman had reigned over three countries at the same time. But your Eminence must know that it is not women who will place me on the Throne, but men—men who will fight for me; men who if necessary will be prepared to die for me.'

Sheena could bear no more. She thought of all the men who had died, the men who were fighting at that very moment, believing their cause to be just and ready to suffer untold hardships that their rightful Queen should return to Scotland and reign over them.

She slipped through the empty ante-chamber and back into the passage. She knew in that moment that the mission on which she had been sent was an utter and complete failure.

She had known without being told that Mary Stuart was

not interested in the stories that she had related of heroism and loyalty, of patriotism and devotion. But she had refused to face the truth, and when the young Queen had changed the subject and talked instead of her gowns and her jewe's, of the party that had been given the night before and the ball they were to attend later in the week, Sheena had tried to excuse her.

'She is so young,' she told herself. 'She is a child dazzled by glittering toys and not really aware of the deep potentialities of life!'

The conversation she had just overheard had not been that of a child but of a woman and, indeed, a woman who knew what she wanted and intended to get it.

Oh, Scotland! Scotland! Her heart went out towards her country, wondering miserably what the future held, wondering how she could ever convey to those who had sent her even a suspicion of the truth.

Without realising it, she had wa'ked along the passage to the top of the great staircase leading down the centre of the Palace, which branched out from the landing, curving gracefully down deep, marble steps to the great hall below. For a moment she stood there looking down and saw in the hall two figures apparently in deep conversation.

At first, intent on her own thoughts, she did not recognise them; then with a little start she realised that the man with his back to the stairs was the Duc, and looking up at him, her head thrown back in an appealing gesture, was the Comtesse René de Pouguet.

The Comtesse was looking her most attractive in the somewhat bold and brazen style she affected, and the long diamond ear-rings glittering in her ears sparkled and swayed against her white neck. She was obviously saying something with great earnestness. and then, as Sheena watched, she put out her hand and laid it affectionately on the Duc's arm, pressing herself momentarily against him as if in that simple gesture she surrendered her whole body to him.

Sheena felt a sudden strange emotion within her own breast. It was almost a pain, as if someone had suddenly stuck a dagger into her heart. For a moment she stared down at the Duc and the Comtesse; then she turned and ran on winged feet to her own bedchamber.

She burst through the door and, finding the room mercifully empty, shut it behind her and turned the key in the lock. Then she leaned against the door panting, her breath coming quickly between her lips, not only from the exertion of running.

For a few seconds she stood there until with a cry that came from the very depths of her being she ran across the room to fling herself headlong, face downwards, on her bed.

Now she recognised and faced the pain that seemed to rend her almost as if it tore her in two. Now she lay feeling and suffering in an agony which was beyond tears.

It was jealousy. She had to face the truth and admit it without hypocrisy and prevarication. Jealousy, which seemed like an evil snake twining itself around her. Jealousy because she loved him!

She had known it, she thought, since the moment he had come to her rescue, as she had stood, bound to the stake, half naked, the flames licking her feet. She had known it as he had covered her with his cloak and lifted her close in his arms. She had known it through the tempest of her tears and in that feeling of utter security and peace as she had ridden home across his saddle.

And, perhaps, she thought now, she had known it even before that. Known it in the sudden feeling of awareness which had come pulsatingly into her throat at the very sight of him. She had thought it was hatred, but she knew now it was a far deeper emotion—a feeling of awareness when a woman is half frightened, half fascinated by the man who is to be her master.

'I love him!'

She whispered the words to herself and knew the very hopelessness of them. Had she not seen the fury and anger

147

in his face the other night when he had shaken her like a child and then kissed her roughly and cruelly with a fire burning fiercely in his eyes? He had no affection for her. She exasperated and annoyed him and he despised her because time after time he had had to rescue her from some unpleasant situation.

Sheena squirmed with humiliation and thought of how the Duc had found the Marquess kissing her in the shadows of the arbour. She remembered again the curl of his lips when she had come running, dishevelled, from the garden and Comte Gustave de Cloude had followed carrying her shawl. She remembered the scorn in his voice as she had entered the inn at Brest that blustery day when she had first set foot in France.

She loved him! It was crazy, ridiculous, impossible, fantastic—and yet it was undeniable. There was no mistaking the arrow that had pierced her as she saw the familiarity with which the Comtesse placed her hand on his arm and the sudden movement of her body towards his.

They were lovers! Sheena was sure of it and yet her whole being cried out in a plea that it might not be so.

She rose suddenly from the bed on which she had flung herself.

'I must go back to Scotland,' she said aloud. 'There is nothing left for me here. I will go back home and try to persuade them that all is well and that Mary Stuart is worthy of their dreams and their aspirations.'

She knew it was a hard, almost impossible task she set herself, and yet, she thought, never would she be instrumental in taking from any man his ideals by which he lived and for which he was prepared to die. Let the Scots go on believing that Mary Stuart cared for them as they cared for her. She would pray that they might never be disillusioned.

There was an expression of stern resolution on Sheena's face as she went to the escritoire and sat down. She picked up her quill and unrolled a piece of parchment.

She would write to her father, she thought, telling him

148

that it was imperative that she returned home immediately. She must at least prepare him for her sudden arrival. Then having dispatched the letter she would go to the coast and hope that she would find a ship in which she could beg a passage.

As she thought of it, she had a sudden yearning for the strength and resilience of the mountains, for the crystal clearness and cleanliness of the burns, for the feeling of the cold, sharp wind from the North Sea on her face, the smell of the heather in her nostrils.

Too long she had been soft; too long she had lingered in a Court that appeared to be concerned only with trivialities, with jousts and tournaments, with balls, routs and masques and all the things which made up the daily programme of amusement for those who must have their senses continually titillated with new sensations.

'I must go home,' Sheena whispered, then knew with a sudden anguish that when she went she would leave her heart behind.

There would never be anyone else in her life, she thought. She knew that instinctively. Ever since she was a child she had dreamed of the man she would one day find and whom she would love with her whole heart, her whole being. She had not imagined him to be in the very least like the Duc. But now she saw that somehow the Duc had taken all the attributes which she had given to the hero of her dreams and had made them his.

She shut her eyes and thought that his handsome, tired, cynical face would be engraved in her memory so that every man on whom she looked would appear to be he. And no other man would have anything to give her, nor wou'd there be anything she could give him because he was not the Duc.

She raised her hands and with the tips of her fingers touched her mouth. He had kissed her. That was something to remember even though the kiss was now but bitter ashes in her mouth.

If only once he could have kissed her gently, a kiss of

friendship or even kindliness, she might have died happy. But instead his kiss had been like a sword—fierce, brutal and cruel; it had left her trembling with a strange flame awakened within herself and which she knew now was love.

'Love is gentle and kind.' She could hear herself repeating the phrase as a schoolchild. It was untrue. Love was cruel and hard and ruthless! A flame which consumed her far more pitiless'y than those which had been lit at her feet by the Reformers.

'I love him! I love him!'

She threw aside her quill and walked restlessly about the room, her silk skirts rustling as she moved across the carpet. She felt as if she walked with naked feet on a bed of thorns.

'I love him! I love him!'

All through the day Sheena kept to her bedchamber, writing the letter to her father, struggling to compose one to the King and another to Mary Stuart in which she thanked them for their hospita'ity and regretted that unavoidable circumstances forced her to return home.

Maggie came to the door and knocked, but she sent her away.

'I have a headache, Maggie, and I want to be alone,' she said, and heard the old maid depart grumblingly and offended that she was not admitted.

Once or twice Sheena went to the window to throw wide the casement and rest her burning cheeks against the diamond panes. She looked out on the quiet, sunlit garden and knew that a battle was taking place within her soul so that for her there was no peace, only war and chaos.

'I love him!'

The sun was sinking when she said it for the thousandth time and realised that her eyes were still dry because she dared not cry at the thought of leaving him behind.

At last, when the shadows were beginning to lengthen, she pulled the bell and summoned Maggie.

'We are leaving for Scotland tomorrow morning,' she said. 'Will you pack my things?'

She saw Maggie's expression of surprise and added:

'Leave behind all the gowns I have been given. They will be of no use to me when I return.'

'Going to Scotland!' Maggie ejaculated. 'Is it bad news ye've received then?'

'Yes, bad news,' Sheena said slowly, thinking nothing could hurt more than the anguish and the loneliness within her.

'I'll do as ye say,' Maggie said, 'and 'tis glad I shall be to be seeing a decent and civilised country again and be talking with decent and civilised folk.'

She was longing to gossip, Sheena knew that, but she turned aside, knowing she could not bear at this moment to hear one of Maggie's juicy bits of scandal which she had heard from the other servants.

There was a knock on the door. Maggie went to open it. She had a long conversation with someone outside, so long that Sheena almost despite herself became curious and called out:

'What is it, Maggie? Who is there?'

Maggie came back into the room carrying a gown in her hand.

' 'Tis a present from Her Majesty Queen Catherine,' she said. 'She asks that you will don it and proceed at once to her apartments. It seems that she is exceedingly anxious to see you for some reason I cannot understand.'

'Te'l Her Majesty that I am slightly indisposed and unable to accept her kind invitation,' Sheena said.

Maggie hesitated a moment before conveying the message, knowing, as Sheena knew, that such a reply would not be well received.

'Do as I say,' Sheena said sharply. 'We go tomorrow. What does it matter what they think tonight?'

She had a sudden revulsion against them all, even against the Queen whom she had been so eager to champion when she had first come to France—'the sleeping panther!' Or

151

was she really just the harmless, ineffectual woman in the background that she appeared to be?

What did it matter? What did any of it matter? Sheena asked herself. She was going away tomorrow. She would be free of them all. In a few years they would only be ghosts at the back of her mind, memories that would amuse her perhaps in the long winter evenings when there was nothing else to do.

She wondered if her father would be pleased to see her —she doubted it. He had very little affection for her, she knew that. His heart and all that was soft and gentle in him was buried in her mother's grave. He had now only a burning patriotism for Scotland, a desire that his country should be rid of the murderous invaders who were destroying not only the financial strength of Scotland but also her manhood.

There would be nobody to welcome her home, Sheena thought, but at least she would not have to pretend. She could sit in the garden and dream of the Duc; she could walk the moors and call his name aloud and no one would hear her but the moorfowl and the gulls coming in from the sea, and he would never know what she felt for him. After a short while he would not even remember the insignificant girl from Scotland whom he had insulted.

Maggie had gone to the door with the gown. When she returned her face was anxious.

'The page seemed to think you had done something which would annoy his Royal mistress,' she announced.

'Tomorrow we shall be gone,' Sheena answered.

'Aye, that's a consolation,' Maggie replied.

She pulled a big trunk from the cupboard. It was worn and battered after the sea journey, but Sheena bent forward to touch it as if it were an old friend.

'Hurry, Maggie,' she said.

In answer Maggie sat back on her heels and looked up at her.

'What is worrying ye?' she said. 'There's something wrong, I can see that sure enough, and haven't I eyes in me

152

head enough to know that ye're unhappy?'

She paused and then added suspiciously:

'What is this news ye've been hearing? Is it from home? Or is it something here that's upset ye?'

Trust Maggie to put her finger on the right spot, Sheena thought.

'You are right,' she said in a weary voice. 'It is something that has upset me here. But, Maggie, I cannot talk of it—not yet. Perhaps later when we are away, when everything is left behind.'

Her voice broke suddenly. She was wondering if after all she could bear the thought of never seeing him again, never hearing his voice, never knowing that sudden thrill and start as he came towards her.

There was so much suffering in her eyes that Maggie turned her face away.

'I suppose ye ken what ye're doing,' she said sourly.

There was a knock at the door, but before Maggie could rise to her feet it opened and a vision of glittering splendour swept into the room. It was the Comtesse René de Pouguet, wearing a gown of emerald-green satin embroidered with diamonds and pearls and her neck and wrists sparkling with the same gems.

She moved imperiously into the middle of the room, and Sheena saw that, following her, was the page carrying the white robe which Maggie had handed back to him.

'Mistress McCraggan,' the Comtesse said and her voice was sharp, 'I sent a page to you a short while ago with an invitation from Her Majesty the Queen. He has returned to say you are indisposed. There appears to me to be little wrong with you.'

'I crave your pardon, Madame,' Sheena said in an attempt at dignity. 'I am not actually ill, but I am in no mood for any type of jollification and I would not inflict my own low spirits on Her Majesty.'

'It is for Her Majesty to judge whether she would be afflicted or not,' the Comtesse replied sharply. 'You are new at Court and therefore I presume must be excused for committing such a *bêtise*. An invitation such as you have received, especially one accompanied by a gift, cannot be refused.'

There was so much scorn in her voice that Sheena flushed nervously.

'I . . . I am sorry . . .' she began, only to be interrupted by the Comtesse saying peremptorily:

'So you should be. I am not accustomed, Mistress Mc-Craggan, to have to interpret Her Majesty's invitations, especially not to persons from other countries who are here as guests of the King.'

Sheena gave a little sigh.

'I apologise,' she said. 'I realise now that it was rude of me and I have no wish to be rude, either to the King or to Her Majesty, who has been most kind.'

'Kind is hardly a strong enough word,' the Comtesse remarked acidly. 'The gowns she has given you amount to a cost of many thousands of francs and I have never known Her Majesty be so gracious, especially to someone of so little importance as yourself.'

Sheena heard Maggie snort indignantly. Because she felt she was in the wrong and that it was undignified to argue further, she merely bowed her head and said quietly:

'You must forgive me for being so ignorant, so ungracious.'

The Comtesse appeared to be mollified a little.

'Fortunately Her Majesty has not been informed of your impertinence,' she said. 'And so I suggest that I merely tell her you have accepted her invitation. Dress quickly, wearing the robe she has sent you as a present, and be in the Royal Apartments within the hour.'

The Comtesse's words were almost like a whip and Sheena suddenly thought that there was something cruel and unpleasant about her beauty and something almost repulsive about her very personality. She wore a heavy, Eastern scent, and when she had gone from the room it seemed to hang ominously in the air, so that on an impulse Sheena crossed to the casement and flung it wide, letting in the evening breeze and the last rays of the setting sun.

'A tartar if ever there was one!' Maggie remarked from behind her. 'And who is she. I should like to know, to give herself such airs and graces? They tell me she was a nobody until she managed to ingratiate herself with the Queen. Thick as thieves, they are, with those sorcerers and soothsayers and all that sort of hanky-panky.'

Sheena made no reply and Maggie went on:

'Ye should hear the things the servants say about her— they know she's of no importance. She set her cap at that *Duc* they say—I canna remember his name but ye know the one I mean. But his valet says that she'll never get him.'

Sheena could not help a sudden lightening of her heart. She tried not to listen, for she knew that nothing she could say would stop Maggie talking.

'There's a lot o' strange things going on,' Maggie continued. 'I canna quite put my finger on it because the Queen's attendants never talk to us lesser fry. They are sort of banded together against the rest of the Palace. But one of the Duchesse's maids was saying to me . . .'

Sheena put her hands over her ears. She could not bear it. She did not want to hear all the chitter-chatter of the stewards' room, of the servants' hall. She wanted to feel free of it all and, most of all, she knew that she wanted to think of the Duc.

She tried not to and yet she could not help it. One part of her body hungered to hear of him, to think of him, to see him; and the other part—her Scottish pride—told her she must forget. If he was not for the Comtesse, he was certainly not for her. Perhaps in Scotland the feel of his lips would leave her mouth; perhaps at home she would no longer be haunted by him. . . .

It was under an hour later that Sheena moved down the passage towards the Queen's apartments. She could see her reflection in the long, gilt mirrors on either side of the passage and she thought she looked like a ghost.

The gown the Queen had sent her was of pure Chinese

155

silk—soft, clinging to her figure and made of such priceless material that one could have drawn it traditionally through a wedding ring. It was pure white and it made her, she thought, look very young and was a striking contrast to the flaming red of her hair.

She had been surprised to find there was no embroidery and no other material used with it, as was the fashion. All the other gowns the Queen had sent her had been heavy with jewe's such as the Queen herself delighted to wear, and there had been insets of velvet and ribbon, satin and lamé, with panels and trains of brocade and waist-bands composed of fine stones.

But this gown was pure and virginal and she wondered if the Queen had particularly wanted her to look young and unsophisticated.

Just for one moment, because she was a woman, Sheena could not help the thought coming into her mind that perhaps the Duc would see her and think her attractive. And then she dismissed the whole idea sternly from her consciousness and told herself that whatever she wore the Duc would look at her only with eyes of fury.

Pages in the Royal livery opened the doub'e doors for her to enter the Queen's apartments and she moved through several ante-chambers until she came to the salon where the Queen habitually received her guests.

It was ill lit this evening. There were not so many tapers as usual in the gold sconces and the crystal chandelier hanging from the ceiling had not been illuminated, which made it difficult to see who was in attendance on Her Majesty.

Everywhere there was the heavy scent of herbs which seemed to Sheena not unlike the incense which was used in church. But it was more pungent, making her feel as if her head was swimming and it was difficult to breathe.

As Sheena entered and the major-domo announced her name she thought that everyone gathered in the room turned towards her as if they had been expecting her entrance. It was a silly impression to have, she thought, and yet she could not help realising there was a sudden silence as she moved towards the Queen, who was seated in a high-backed chair and curtsied low before her.

The Queen held out her hand and she kissed the white fingers, noticing as she did so that they were hot and a little wet. Sheena felt a sudden revulsion. What was it about the Queen, she wondered, which struck her now as unpleasant?

It was not only that she was dirty and there was a faint aroma about her which even the use of heavy perfumes could not disguise. There was something else, Sheena thought, something in the whole room which made her feel as if her hackles were rising.

She glanced round. The Marquess was there, the Comtesse René de Pouguet and several other people whose faces she recognised vaguely but to whom she could not put a name.

'We are glad you are here, Mistress McCraggan,' the Queen said, with her Italian accent very noticeable. 'You have not dined?'

'No, indeed,' Sheena said. 'In fact, your Majesty, I have not eaten all day. I have forgotten about it until now.'

The Queen smiled. It seemed to Sheena as if she was unnaturally pleased at the news.

'That is very good! Very good!' she said. 'Well, we will eat later. First we will drink.'

She made a gesture with her hands towards the pages, who came forward with gold trays on which there were crystal glasses filled with dark-red wine. They offered the tray to the Queen and to the other guests and then another page came towards Sheena holding a gold salver on which there was one glass—a beautifully chased goblet set with emeralds and diamonds.

'A special glass of wine for you, Mistress McCraggan,' the Queen said.

'I am sorry, your Majesty,' Sheena answered, 'but I never drink wine.'

The Queen's face darkened.

'It is a loving-cup between friends,' she expostulated; 'we should take it most amiss if you were to refuse.'

'O . . . of course, your Majesty,' Sheena stammered.

She put out her hand towards the goblet. She did not know why, but she had a curious reluctance to take it. She had a feeling deep in her heart that something was wrong; and yet she knew it was absurd and the Queen was just showing her usual kindness.

Remembering that she had not yet thanked Her Majesty for the gown she was wearing, Sheena said quickly:

'I must thank you, Ma'am, for your most kind and generous present. As you see, it fits me perfectly.'

'I thought it would,' the Queen said. 'You look very lovely, my dear.' She turned her head towards the Marquess. 'Do you not agree with me, my Lord?'

As if the Marquess had been waiting for a cue so that he could join in the conversation, he moved from behind the Queen's chair to Sheena's side. He raised her hand to his lips and looking down into her eyes said:

'You are as lovely as a Vestal Virgin or, indeed, as any of the nymphs who were once pursued by the gods from Olympus.'

As always when she was paid a fu'some compliment Sheena was embarrassed. She tried to pull her hand away from the Marquess's fingers, but he grasped her intention and, laughing a little beneath his breath, bent and kissed it again.

'The Scots do not know how to take a compliment,' he said tauntingly.

'We like them only when they are completely sincere,' Sheena retorted, and they all laughed as if she had said something very witty.

'Drink the wine,' the Queen said, 'and then we have something to do which I think will amuse you.'

'What is that?' Sheena enquired.

The Queen's eyes seemed to light up.

'You have never seen my tower. I built it at the side of the Palace so that my soothsayers could communicate with the heavens and could read for me the secrets of the stars.'

'I . . . I have heard of it, your Majesty,' Sheena said, striving to be polite.

'Many people talk of it,' the Queen replied, 'but few are privileged to go inside. Only my very special friends are invited.'

She smiled at the assembled throng. Sheena clutched the goblet in her hand and wondered once again why she felt so uneasy, why there was a strange premonition within her that something was wrong.

The Queen indicated the goblet in Sheena's hand and the Marquess raised his own glass.

'Let me give you a toast,' he said. 'To the unknown and the future, whatever it may bring us!'

The other guests held up their g'asses.

'To the unknown!' they echoed.

Sheena realised the Queen was watching her. She put the goblet to her lips. The metal felt cold and as if in contrast the wine itself seemed almost warm. Blood warmth, she thought, and wondered why the words came to her mind.

'Drink! Drink it up!' The Queen had bent forward in her chair. 'It is for you. A sign of my favour; a token of my affection, Mistress McCraggan. Drink it up!'

There was nothing Sheena could do but tip the goblet up, feeling the wine flow down her throat, almost, she thought, like a river in spate. It was not unpleasant and because the Queen was watching her she drank the contents of the goblet almost to the bottom.

Then she turned to put it down, looking for a table or a page standing near with a tray in his hand. And even as she did so she realised that everyone was watching her. There was silence in the room, a heavy, ominous silence as if everyone ceased breathing and she could only see their eyes.

Eyes! Eyes! Everywhere! Watching her! Staring at her! For a moment she thought she must have gone deaf; they must be talking and she could not hear them.

And then almost like smoke rising from a fire she felt a wave rising up through her body towards her brain—dark, sinister and evil. She could feel it seeping its way through her, rising, rising until it reached the very top of her head and she knew a sudden blackness was encompassing her.

She made one last frantic effort to clear her senses, to turn and run from the room. But it was too late! The waves of darkness caught up with her, splashed over her and she felt herself sinking down, until she knew no more.

11

Something was struggling. Out of the darkness which seemed impenetrable a faint light came and went, hardly larger than a pinpoint, growing nearer and then receding.

There was a noise—a noise of chanting voices and a deeper note of someone exalting and declaiming. That too receded and there was only darkness again; a darkness, however, of which one was conscious, knowing it to be evil.

Strange words were being cried aloud; names which seemed vaguely familiar and yet at the same time repellent.

Slowly, as if she came back from a very, very long distance, Sheena heard chanting. It was in a language she recognised as Latin but the words did not make sense.

'*Quotidianeum panem nostrum hodie nobis da. . . .*'

Could it be? It sounded like the Lord's Prayer said backwards, but her numbed brain could not hold the thought. There was the heavy, sickly smell of incense. It seemed to fill her nostrils and suffocate her. But after a long time, when the voices receded, came back and receded again, she had a sudden fear of what was being said and knew that she could no longer go on listening.

She must move; she must go away. She could no longer

eavesdrop on what was happening because she knew it to be wrong and wicked. She tried to move and realised, in a sudden terror such as she had never felt before in the whole of her life, that she was paralysed.

Her limbs were like lead weighing her down, utterly divorced from her mind; and yet she was conscious of them. Her feet, her legs, her arms, her body and her breasts —she knew they were there but they were no longer under her control.

She struggled and yet she did not move. She fought against the paralysis that was all the more terrifying because she could only fight it mentally. She thought that she must open her lips and cry out in her terror, but her lips were motionless and her voice was silent in her throat.

It was then that she thought she must be dead; and yet if this was death to what sort of place had she been carried? The intonations grew louder:

'*Malo nos libera sed. . . .*'

She knew now that the voices were all around her. They came from the front, the back and the sides—a circle and she was in the middle of it.

Sheena struggled again and knew the utter helplessness of being a prisoner, though no bonds and no chains were required but only the refusal of her own body to obey the commands she gave it.'

'I must go! I must!'

She knew that she could not.

Still the voices went on. She tried to open her eyes, but the lids would not raise themselves and she felt them heavy over her pupils—so heavy they seemed to weigh her down so that she must sink away into the darkness from which she had emerged.

She fought against the complete blackness which was threatening to overcome her again. She felt choked and nauseated by the incense; and there was something else too, something cruel and evil hovering just outside her consciousness, something which seemed to her as if it were waiting to capture her.

'Lord Satan, hear us!' a man's voice chanted in French.
'Master of Darkness, come to us!' came the response.

The voices rose in a shrill crescendo, and now Sheena's brain cleared a little and she could hear more distinctly the deep, resonant voice of a man who seemed to be standing directly above her while the responses came from those on either side.

She knew now that she was lying flat on her back, her face turned upwards. There was evil, evil and danger all around her. She could sense it as an animal senses danger.

It seemed to her that beyond the intonation and the responses there was the flutter as of great wings, perhaps dark and hooked ones like those of a bat. She tried to scream again and the very effort brought her nearer to the darkness which seemed to be pulling at her with crooked claws.

She began to pray.

'God save me! Save me from this whatever it may be. Keep the evil from me. Save me! Oh, save me, God!'

Blindly, like a child reaching out towards its mother, her frightened mind sought for a symbol and found it in the thought of the cross. She could see it quite clearly behind her closed eyes—a cross of light, golden and shining, which seemed from the moment it appeared to drive away some of the darkness, to draw her from the hands that would have held her back.

'Our Father which art in Heaven . . .'

It was the prayer she had learnt as a child; the prayer she had said all her life when she went to bed and when she awoke in the morning. Her lips did not move, but she said it fervently in her heart.

'. . . and deliver us from evil . . .'

It seemed to her that she was crying the words aloud and now, almost as if her prayer was answered, she felt a faint lightening of her heavy eyelids.

'. . . Amen. Amen.'

Slowly, for one flickering moment, her eyes opened, then closed again. There was only a fraction of a second in which she could see before the heaviness descended once more; and she felt it would be a superhuman task to raise her lids again and she was not capable of it.

In that moment she had seen enough to make her lie faint and terrified in a panic that was beyond expression. She felt that she must doubt what she had seen and that it could be nothing but a dream; then, as the cross still remained before her closed eyelids, she knew it was the truth.

She was lying naked, her body white as alabaster, upon a black velvet altar. There were seven great lighted black candles beyond her feet, and she knew, though she could not see them, that there must be six behind her head. Above her was the crucifix, but it was upside down!

The Black Mass! The intonations in Latin—now she understood. The prayers were being said backwards.

Kneeling, staring at her as they responded to the exaltation of the priest or sorcerer who stood beside her, were the Queen and her friends.

Sheena could recognise the Queen's voice now, hear the Italian accent in the pronunciation of her words and hear, too, the sensuous excitement in her tones.

Suddenly with a sick horror Sheena knew what was happening. They were in the tower—the tower the Queen had built for her sorcerers and necromancers; the tower of which many strange things were reported.

Black magic! They were words to make the strongest man tremble; words from which decent women shuddered and turned away.

Sheena remembered that Maggie had hinted at the many strange rites and ceremonies which were reported to have taken place in the tower. No one was allowed there save the Queen's most intimate cronies; but servants talked and they told of broken pieces of wax images in which were stuck hundreds of pins; of frogs and bats and newts which had been asked for by the sorcerers; of snakes which required strange food to keep them alive; and sacrifices. . . .

Sheena stopped thinking and felt as if a ghostly hand

clutched at her throat. Sacrifices! Was that what she was to be? A sacrifice. Killed so that the blood of the victim could bring satanic power to those who drank it.

Again she tried to scream and knew that no sound came from her lips. A sacrifice for what? All the Palace knew why the Queen paid her sorcerers and why she sent far and wide for other and cleverer ones. There was only one thing she desired—to destroy the Duchesse and her spell over the King.

'If anything would convince me that the devil does not exist,' Sheena had heard one courtier say sneeringly, 'it would be the Queen's inability to make any impact on the Duchesse's youth and beauty despite her continual prayers to Satan himself.'

She had thought it just a figure of speech at the time, but now she knew it was the truth. The Queen was in league with Satan. She was evoking his aid, calling upon him to destroy her enemy, promising him her heart and her soul if only she could harness the forces of darkness and destroy the Duchesse's power over the King.

Sheena remembered how the Queen had sent for her and commanded her to appear in a gown of virginal whiteness. How easy to understand now her plan and how cleverly it had been executed. No wonder the Comtesse had swept aside her efforts to refuse the invitation.

With an effort which felt as if she were raising great tons of steel, Sheena raised her eyelids a fraction. Through her eye-lashes she could see a cloud of incense and the Comtesse's face emerging, as it were, through a purple-and-green fog. She was staring upwards with a look of intense concentration and her mouth was shut in a narrow, evil line.

'It cannot be so important for her to destroy the Duchesse as for the Queen,' Sheena thought, and saw then the Queen's face, her eyes protruding with a rapture that was unmistakable, her mouth wet and half open, her hands clenched beneath her chin, as if in prayer, until the knuckles showed white.

'The sleeping panther wakes!' Sheena almost felt as if she heard the words said in her ear, and then just before her eyelids closed from the strain and exhaustion of trying to prop them open, she glanced again at the Comtesse and wondered on what object her whole being was concentrated.

Almost like a clap of thunder she knew the answer. The Comtesse was praying that she might possess the Duc even as the Queen prayed to possess the King.

As if someone screamed the words aloud, Sheena felt her whole being yearning for the one man who could save her, the one man who had come to her rescue before and who she knew must be her saviour now.

'Come to me! Save me! Help me! Hear me!'

She felt her cry winging its way through the darkness towards him.

'Oh, God, make him hear me! Oh, God, let him think of me and know that I am in danger!'

She was praying to the cross which once more she could see against her closed eyelids. She was praying with an intensity that somehow she knew was the only thing which would keep her from slipping back into the darkness which even now advanced and receded like great waves over her tortured mind.

'I am paralysed. Will I ever move again? Even if I cannot, save what is left of me. Come to me.'

She felt that he must hear her, must know that she was in need of him simply because her need was so great.

And now the chanting and the voices around her were rising, shriller and shriller, deeper and more intense, and she heard the movements of the sorcerer—a sudden scraping of something which creaked a little as if it were a basket, the rustle of wings which tried to fly and were prevented, and the frightened cry of a cock.

She knew then that she was not to be the sacrifice. Instead the cock was to be sacrificed over her bared body and in her mind she twisted and turned, struggled and fought against the bestiality of it. But she knew that in reality not

165

one muscle of her drugged body moved and she could only lie there, humiliated by her nakedness, and hear the sudden shriek of the voices as the thrill and excitement of the service reached its climax.

Just for one moment she strove to open her eyes, saw the black cock flapping and fluttering above her, caught a glimpse of the light shining on the sharpness of the knife as it severed the bird's head from its body and the red blood as it came pouring down over her breasts and stomach.

It was then that she must have fainted or have let the darkness which was hovering so near to her mind encompass it, for she knew no more. She only knew that the evil that was being evoked was close to her, a very real, a very threatening, thing; something cruel and horrible, with great wings shaped like a bat's.

It was coming nearer, nearer and nearer, to accept the sacrifice, to take it from those who offered it. And then as Sheena was lost in the darkness she knew the cross was still there, protecting and holding her. . . .

It must have been a long time later that her tired mind struggled back into consciousness. Now the chanting and the exaltation had finished and the incense had died down to remain only a fragrance on the air. Someone was sponging her body clean of the blood and drying her with a soft towel.

She tried to move and found that her body was still paralysed—and yet there was feeling in it. She could feel the black velvet beneath her; she could feel that the unseen hands which had sponged her were now covering her nakedness with something silken and she could hear voices talking in low but normal tones.

'Will you carry her?' she heard the Queen ask, and heard the Marquess reply:

'Of course, Madame. She is no weight and anyway it is not far.'

'We must be careful,' the Queen said in a low voice.

'I will go and find out what is happening,' the Comtesse volunteered.

It was not hard to recognise her voice. There was something insidious and snakelike about it, something, Sheena thought, which should have warned her from the very first moment that they met that the Comtesse was not to be trusted.

'Your Majesty is satisfied?'

It was the voice of the sorcerer, the man who stood beside her and who Sheena knew had killed the cock.

'You were magnificent, Ruggieri,' the Queen replied. 'Tonight I felt our lord and master nearer than I have ever known him before.'

'I, too, was conscious of his presence,' the sorcerer said, 'so I cannot but be certain that your Majesty's aspirations will be realised.'

'I am sure of it,' the Queen said. 'Take this ring. It is a paltry award for your services, but you understand that the thankfulness with which it is given comes from the depths of my heart.'

'I am deeply honoured, your Majesty.'

He moved away. Sheena could hear him go, and now the Queen said in a low voice to the Marquess:

'You are sure that the King was attracted by her?'

'Most certainly, Madame. How could he fail to be? Is she not fair-skinned with the same red hair that has bewitched him for so many years?'

'Yes, they are not unlike,' the Queen said.

'What is more, Lady Fleming was of the same colour.'

'That is true, that is true,' the Queen muttered. 'We have been over this so often, my Lord Marquess, and yet I need to be reassured.'

'How could you question anything after what you have just experienced?' the Marquess asked softly.

His words sounded sincere and yet listening to them with closed eyes Sheena could hear the cynicism and hypocrisy behind them even while the Queen was satisfied.

'You are so kind,' she murmured, 'and you shall not

167

go unrewarded. I shall never forget all that you have done for me.'

'All I ask, Madame. is to be your most obedient servant,' the Marquess said, and Sheena felt that the Queen must be deaf not to hear the sneer in the words.

'I am so grateful to you all,' the Queen said. 'So very, very grateful for your loyalty and the comfort you have given me. One day the King will return to me—but only if that woman is dead.'

'Or if His Majesty's affections are engaged elsewhere,' the Marquess said silkily.

'Yes, that is my hope. Who knows that tonight may not be the turning point, the moment when the Duchesse's power ebbs away because another holds the King's fancy.'

Sheena listened in bewilderment. What was expected of this orgy of evil? For what particular reason had they evoked the powers of Satan?

The drug was still threatening to paralyse her brain as it paralysed her body. She lost the thread of the conversation between the Queen and the Marquess and heard only the voice of the Comtesse as she came gliding over the room to say in excited tones:

'His Majesty has gone to the Duchesse's apartments. He has not been there more than ten minutes.'

'We must move quickly,' the Queen said.

Sheena heard the Marquess take a step forward, she felt his hands pass under her inert body and lift her in his arms. She would have cried out then at the indignity of it, in knowing that he touched her nakedness, but she was as help'ess as a piece of driftwood battered in the waves of a stormy sea.

He lifted her and someone—she thought it was the Comtesse—threw part of the silken shroud which covered her over her face. Then another heavier cloth was added. She was covered completely and she heard the Marquess say:

'If I meet anyone in the corridor it will be hard to see what I am carrying.'

'Where are they taking me?' Sheena wondered in a

sudden anguish. 'Where can they be taking me?'

She thought fearfully that they might be going to destroy her. Were they about to bury her alive or cast her into some deep lake or pool from which her body could never be recovered? Was the sacrifice, once it had been made, of little use thereafter?

She struggled to remember; but her mind felt as if it would no longer function, and she could only lie half suffocated by the clothes that covered her face and by the terror within her heart.

'Go, and the Prince of Darkness go with you!' she heard the Queen say, and instinctively groped within herself for the cross that had kept her safe so far.

Now the Marquess was carrying her down the passage. She could feel him move slowly, burdened by her weight, and she knew that the Comtesse walked beside him because she could hear the rustle of her gown and the quickness of her breathing as if she were afraid.

They had not got very far when Sheena heard the Comtesse give an almost inarticulate cry and knew that her hand went out to clutch the Marquess's arm.

'Who is it?' he asked.

' 'Tis the Duc de Salvoire,' came the whispered reply.

She was saved! Sheena felt her whole being cry out in thankfulness, in the utter relief of knowing that he had come. He must have heard her prayers and her cry for help and now he was here.

'Good evening, Jarnac!'

The Comtesse's voice was light and Sheena realised that they must be face to face with the Duc.

She fancied she could hear his footsteps on the thick carpet.

'Your servant, René!'

He must be bowing and Sheena could hear the rustle of the Comtesse's gown as she curtsied.

'Shall we see you later at the gaming-table?'

The Comtesse's voice was gay and enticing.

'Perhaps.'

The Duc was noncommittal and Sheena fancied that he was looking at the Marquess, staring perhaps at her. She tried to move, struggling to raise her hand so that she could pull the silk coverings from her face.

'Where are you going?' the Duc asked with a touch of suspicion in his voice. 'And why has our nob'e Marquess been turned into a beast of burden? Surely there are servants in the Palace?'

The Duc was being deliberately provocative. Sheena could hear it in his voice. Did he suspect that she was there? she wondered. With a sudden feeling of horror she thought that perhaps he did not suspect; that the Duc was merely being unpleasant because he disliked the Marquess.

'You are not to ask questions,' the Comtesse replied quickly before the Marquess could answer. 'We are on the Queen's business. This is a very special present that she has for the King and she would entrust it to no one save the Marquess himself.'

'How perceptive of Her Majesty!'

There was no disguising the contempt in the Duc's voice. For a moment no one answered and he continued:

'I must not keep you. I wait upon the Duchesse de Valentinois.'

'Do not go! Do not go!' Sheena cried out to him in her heart and knew in terror that her lips could not say anything.

'Wait! Wait! I am here!' she called and heard, with a sinking of her heart, the Duc's footsteps going away down the corridor.

'Do you think he suspected?'

The Marquess spoke almost in a whisper.

'He had no idea,' the Comtesse replied. 'You might be carrying anything. He will not think of it again.'

'The man always turns up when he is not wanted,' the Marquess said savagely.

'There is no need to be afraid of him,' the Comtesse said. 'I will find him and keep him engaged for the rest of the evening. Let us hurry. One would think people had something better to do than to walk the corridors at this time of night.'

'Especially these particular corridors,' the Marquess muttered.

They went a little further and then Sheena heard a door open and a man's voice ask:

'Who is it?'

It must be one of the grooms of the chamber, she thought, for most of them came from Normandy and were engaged by the Duchesse and his voice had a particularly Norman accent.

'It is a present that the Queen has sent His Majesty,' the Comtesse explained again. 'A very special present—and Her Majesty's instructions are that we are to leave it in the bed-chamber so that he will find it later in the evening.'

The groom had obviously recognised the Comtesse, for he said:

'Very good, m'Lady,' and Sheena heard another door open.

Now, at last, she realised what was happening. She felt herself carried across a large chamber and laid down on the softness of a bed and she understood that the Comtesse had told the truth. She was, indeed, a present for the King —a present to be left waiting for him in his bedchamber when he should retire for the night.

The full horror of what had happened and what was still happening came to her so brutally that she felt as if she might die of the shock of it. She felt the Marquess lay her down, felt him or the Comtesse draw first the heavy shroud and then the silken one from her face and body.

Then, utterly naked, she lay in the King's bed and was covered by the King's sheets.

'She looks very young,' she heard the Marquess say, and his voice was thick with lust.

'Let us hope that is what he will find attractive about her,' the Comtesse said. 'Old women must pall in time even on the most devoted of men, and the Duchesse is old!'

She almost spat the words out.

'You hate her, do you not?' the Marquess said, as if he had realised it for the first time.

'Yes, I hate her,' the Comtesse answered. 'The Duc admires her, finds her completely irresistible. Is not that enough to make me hate her? But he will be mine after tonight, I am sure of it.'

'You believe all that rubbish?' the Marquess asked.

'Rubbish?' the Comtesse queried. 'Did you not feel something strong, powerful, that we evoked with our prayers and by the sacrifice? It was there, I know it. I could feel it hovering over me. He had come at last after so many attempts to bring him had failed.'

'I felt nothing,' the Marquess said, half angrily, and yet, Sheena thought, with a touch of doubt in his voice. 'The Queen is crazed to believe in it and so are you.'

'Crazed or not, tonight there was something there,' the Comtesse whispered.

'All I saw was a very lovely naked girl,' the Marquess replied, forcing himself, Sheena thought, to talk normally because he was half afraid of his own thoughts. 'If I thought the King was to be delayed for long I might substitute for him. I am certain I would prove a far more ardent and far more persuasive lover.'

As he spoke Sheena felt his hand upon the bedclothes, but the Comtesse gave a little cry.

'Leave her alone! Do not dare touch her. She is dedicated. The sacrifice has been made on her. She is for one person and one person only and I know, whatever you may say, that the power within her will draw the King like a magnet will draw a piece of steel. Come away! Come away quickly! We must not be found here!'

'I am coming.'

The Marquess's voice was sulky. Sheena heard them moving away and the door closed behind them.

She lay there in an agony that was beyond words. To know what was happening and to be unable to move. To fight against the paralysis which held her limbs rigid and

172

her lips silent was a torture such as only some monster of cruelty could have devised.

She fought and fought against her own weakness and frailty; and then, knowing that every effort was inadequate and hopeless, resorted once more to prayer.

'God help me! How could he have passed me by? How could he have been so close and not known? Make him realise that he must come to me. Let him hear this wherever he may be, whoever he is with. Turn him again in this direction.'

How long she prayed she did not know, but when she ceased through sheer and utter exhaustion she realised that her eyes were open. For the first time she looked on the King's bedchamber, seeing in the light of two small tapers which were lit in the sconces that she was lying in a great four-poster bed with embroidered hangings and carved posts.

The rest of the room was in darkness. The windows overlooked the garden and she could feel a faint breeze blowing in as the curtains were swayed by it.

'What can I do?' Sheena thought agonisingly. She tried to turn from one side to the other, tried to move her feet, her fingers, but only her eyes were free. The drug was wearing off, she thought, because her brain was clearer; but the darkness of unconsciousness was not very far away and she guessed it would be some time before she could really move or cry out.

Perhaps her voice would be the last thing to come to her; and if it was how could she ever explain to the King why she was there or beg him not to take advantage of her? What would he think when he found her naked between his sheets, her head lying on his pillow?

'I must do something. I must do something,' she thought, and knew in desperation that there was nothing left for her but prayer.

Her eyes were closed and she was praying again, praying with an intensity which seemed as difficult as if she moved a great weight from off the ground.

'God help me! God help me!'

She heard the door of the bedchamber open and the words died in her mind. She dared not open her eyes. There was someone in the room. Would he see her at once, she wondered, or would he begin to undress and then realise her presence?

She still dared not open her eyes; but now, for the first time, she could feel a movement in her breasts. She could feel them moving tumultuously; she could feel her breath coming quickly. Still there was no voice in her throat.

Someone was coming towards her! And now he had reached the bed and was standing there. What would he say? she wondered. Would he ask her what was her business?

She lay in a terror so agonising that she knew that if she were not paralysed she would be shaking all over. And then because she could bear it no longer, because she must face up to whatever lay waiting for her, she opened her eyes, prepared to plead, if not with her lips then with her soul, for mercy.

Slowly she looked upwards and then with a sudden leap of her heart saw that it was not the King standing there but the Duc. He was staring down at her, but the expression on his face was hidden in the shadow of the curtains.

'You have come! You have come!' she wanted to say. 'Take me away. Take me away quickly. Hide me. Oh, thank God, you have come!'

'What are you doing here?'

She heard his voice, deep and low, as if it came from a long distance.

She struggled to answer him, but knew that her lips would not move.

'I could hardly credit it could be true,' she heard the Duc say. 'But your maid told me that you had gone to the Queen, that she had sent you a gown of white, plain and unembroidered. What has happened? Are you bewitched? Or are you here of your own free will?'

174

Sheena could not move. She could only stare at him, her eyes wide in her pale face.

'Do you wish me to take you away?' he asked. 'Tell me or else I must leave you to do as they wish. Answer me.'

She could only feel her breasts moving beneath the silk sheets.

'What is the matter with you?' he asked. 'Why can you not tell me if they have put a spell upon you or if, indeed, you have merely acquiesced in their wishes.'

She looked up at him, willing him to understand.

'I suppose your silence means that you have agreed to do this thing,' he said, and would have turned away.

She saw that he was going and knew that her last hope had gone. The terror and fear of it was unbearable and as he moved away from the bed she made a sound, strangled, like an animal in pain, but at least a sound.

He turned back and now a tear was running from the corner of her eye, down her cheek. He stared down at her.

'Is it possible?' he muttered almost to himself.

He threw back the sheet, took her hand in his and raising her arm released it. It fell back with an inanimate thud on the bed.

'My God!'

The words were through clenched teeth and now he stripped the sheet from the bed and wrapped it round her. Then he lifted her in his arms. For a moment he stared down at her and in the light of the tapers she saw an expression on his face that she had never seen there before.

'That they should have done this to you,' he said. 'My God, they shall pay for it!'

His arms seemed to tighten about her.

'My love! My poor little love!' she thought she heard him say, but she could not be certain because now she knew she need no longer struggle and fight she slipped away into the peace of a gentle unconsciousness in which there was no terror and no evil.

175

12

Someone was shaking her, rocking her backwards and forwards, and for a moment her mind caught at an echo, remembering that it had happened to her before. Then with an effort so intense that it was actually a physical pain Sheena came back to consciousness.

It was Maggie who was shaking her; Maggie who had her hands on her shoulders and was saying in a low, insistent voice:

'Wake up, ma bairn, wake up! 'Tis of import.'

'What is it, Maggie?'

Sheena tried to say the words drowsily and heard them coming jerkily from her lips as Maggie continued to shake her into wakefulness.

'God be praised ye're awake and in your full senses,' Maggie said, more as if she reassured herself by the latter statement than because she was unduly convinced of it.

'What is the matter?' Sheena asked wonderingly.

Her head felt soft and woolly and now as she opened her eyes she found the candles were lit and that Maggie was wearing her shawl and bonnet. She forced herself to sit up in bed.

'What time is it?' she asked. 'And why are you dressed like that?'

'Because we are going awa',' Maggie said briefly.

Sheena passed her fingers over her forehead and through the curls clustering around it, and then, like a child, she put her knuckles in her eyes.

'I am sleepy, Maggie,' she complained. 'So sleepy that I cannot understand what you are saying.'

'Wake up!' Maggie almost hissed the words. 'We have got to be awa'.'

Sheena took her hands from her face and stared at Maggie in astonishment. As she did so she suddenly remembered. It came back to her slowly, almost as if someone opened a book page by page—the wine she had drunk in the Queen's apartments; the expression on the Marquess's face; another awakening; the intonation and chanting of those who evoked the devil.

She gave a shiver at the thought and put her hands to her throat. That is what they had been doing, evoking the devil in the Black Mass over her naked body, and then they had carried her, paralysed, unable to move, down to the King's bed.

In a sudden terror Sheena stretched out her arms—she could move; and her legs—she could feel them. She threw back the bedclothes and stepped on to the floor. For a moment she swayed because her head felt strange and because her limbs would not obey her.

'I can move! Maggie, I can move again!'

Her relief was almost like a paean of thanksgiving, but Maggie was not listening. She had turned to the chair and was bringing Sheena her shift.

'Get dressed, Mistress, for the love of Heaven. There's no time to be lost.'

'I am saved! I am saved!' Sheena wanted to cry aloud and then she remembered who had saved her and a sudden joy shot through her, clearing her mind, sweeping away the feeling of faintness and inertia.

'Hurry! Hurry!'

Maggie's voice intruded so that she was forced to pay attention.

'What is it, Maggie?' she asked. 'Surely it is not time to rise.'

Without waiting for an answer she moved across the room and pulled back the curtains. Outside there was only the dark sable of the sky and the stars were twinkling overhead.

'It is still night!' Sheena exclaimed.

'We have got to leave,' Maggie answered. 'The Lord have mercy on us but can I not get it into your head that we're in danger? "Terrible danger" was what His Grace said.'

177

'His Grace?' Sheena asked the question sharply.

Maggie nodded.

'He brought ye here, more dead than alive,' she answered. 'He gave me his orders and because I know he was speaking the truth I'm going to carry them out. Get your clothes on, bairn, there's no time for talking.'

Danger! That was a word Sheena understood only too well by now. Quickly she slipped on the clothes Maggie handed her, washed her face and hands in cold water and took her bonnet from Maggie's ever-ready hand.

It was then for the first time that she noticed that the trunks were strapped ready in the centre of the room.

'You have packed!' she exclaimed.

'A fine muddle everything is in,' Maggie retorted, 'but I wasna leaving anything behind.'

'And where are we going?' Sheena asked, as she pulled a fur-lined cloak around her shoulders. It was only as she did so that she remembered who had made her a present of such a magnificent garment, but even as the thought flashed through her mind Maggie answered her question and drove everything else from it.

'Home,' she said. 'Home to Scotland. Does that make ye happy?'

'Going home!' Sheena repeated stupidly.

'Aye, and the carriage is waiting for us downstairs. Wait while I call the footmen who are outside to collect our trunks.'

'Maggie, what . . . I do not understand . . .'

Sheena's voice died away, for Maggie, without waiting for what she was about to say, hurried to the door. Two flunkies entered and one glance at them was enough for Sheena to know by their livery who was their master.

It was the Duc who had arranged all this; the Duc who had rescued her last night and was now sending her away to safety, sending her home. She should have been delighted and thrilled, she knew that. Had this not been what she wanted ever since she came to France?—to go back to Scotland; to be in her own land amongst things

178

and people who were familiar and a part of her own life.

And yet now the moment had come there was something else which swept away all gladness, all joy, at the thought. It was then with a little sob she realised that if she went now she would leave her heart behind.

'Maggie, Maggie, I cannot . . .' she began to say in a trembling voice, but already it was too late. The footmen had carried her trunks from the room and Maggie, snatching up a shawl that had been forgotten and with a quick glance round, took her by the hand and drew her forward to follow them.

'But, Maggie, I cannot go . . .' she expostulated again, only to be hushed into silence.

'Dinna speak,' Maggie commanded in a whisper. 'No one must know you are leaving, do ye not understand? Ye're in danger, bairn; terrible danger is what he said.'

As Maggie repeated the Duc's words the full import of them sank into Sheena's brain. Of course she was in danger, she could see that now. She had been chosen by the Queen for a special purpose and because her project had not succeeded Her Majesty would have no mercy on the person who had failed her.

Besides, she knew too much. Sheena had lived long enough at Court to realise that those with an unhealthy knowledge of persons more powerful than themselves were invariably in grave danger. Sometimes they fell sick and died of some mysterious disease. Sometimes they were accused of peculiar and unsubstantiated crimes and were taken to prison never to return.

Whatever the course adopted, the offending person was skilfully and cleverly eliminated. What chance had she, knowing what she did, having seen what she had seen and having, through the Duc's intervention, escaped at the last moment unscathed from the King's bed?

She was silent, therefore, as Maggie led her swiftly down the passages, many of them almost in darkness as the tapers flickered in their grease or went out altogether. The Palace was sleeping and yet Sheena fancied there were a thousand strange noises she had never heard before—the creak of the floor-boards; the muffled sounds behind closed doors; the whisper of the wind against the windows; and above it all the thumping of her heart.

There was the smell, too, of something acrid and frightening, as if she could breathe in her own fear and know it permeated all the rest of the party with her. Every moment Sheena expected someone to burst out of one of the doors they passed and come hurrying after them down the long corridors, calling them to stop, demanding in the Queen's name that she return to her room—then waiting there for the sentence of death to be passed upon her.

And would death from the Queen and those who served her be a quick and merciful one? Sheena doubted it. She could see again the glint of evil in their eyes as she raised the goblet of wine to her lips. That was what it had been and yet at the time she had not recognised it.

She could hear again the evil of their voices as they called up the malevolent spirits in which they believed. Danger! Danger! She could hear the Duc's voice, long, long ago it seemed to her, saying that very word, and she had not believed him.

At last they reached the courtyard. It was one that she had never visited before, small and unobtrusive and obviously in the less important parts of the Palace; perhaps somewhere near the vast kitchens, for there was refuse and old wine bottles tumbled about outside and hungry cats stalking in the shadows.

A coach was waiting and already the flunkies were lifting her trunks on to the roof and Maggie was helping her up the step and through the door into the soft-cushioned interior.

There was no need for Sheena to look at the emblazoned coat-of-arms which decorated the panels to know to whom it belonged. One glance at the six horses which pulled it, with their crested harnesses and nodding head-plumes, was enough. It was the Duc's coach. It was the Duc who was sending her to safety.

They were off. The coachmen turned the horses; Sheena felt them drive slowly through the gateway of the courtyard and then the speed was increasing, the wheels were flying round, the hoofs were ringing out on the cobbles of the empty streets.

'Thank the Lord we're awa'!' Maggie said, and there was such a heartfelt cry of relief in her voice that instinctively Sheena put her hand over her maid's to comfort her.

'We are safe enough, Maggie,' she said, 'if the Duc has the care of us.'

'I was afeared they wou'd stop us,' Maggie said, and Sheena saw the tears in her eyes and heard the break in her voice.

'What did . . . he say to you?' Sheena enquired, and there was no need to ask whom she meant.

'He brought ye into the bedchamber in his arms,' Maggie said. 'For a wee moment I thought ye were dead, and then, as he laid ye down on the bed and put the covers over ye with the gentleness of a woman, he said: "We have got to get your mistress away—now, at once, tonight. Do you understand?"

'I didna answer and he went on: "Your mistress is in danger, terrible danger. If she stays here she will die, or even a worse fate might befall her." '

Sheena drew a deep breath. She knew full well what the Duc meant. Maggie suddenly took her handkerchief from her sleeve and mopped her eyes.

'It seemed as if I'd never get the things packed,' she said. ' "Leave your mistress until the last moment," he told me, and I obeyed because of the way he said it and all the time I was afeared I would be too s'ow, too late.'

Maggie gave a little sob and Sheena put her arm around her shoulders.

'It is all right, Maggie,' she said. 'It is all over now.'

'Is it?' Maggie asked. 'Not until we're out of this accursed country. They may come after ye. They've got soldiers, and men on horseback can ride faster than we can travel, even with all these horses.'

'We have got a start on them, anyway,' Sheena said soothingly.

She realised that the coach had been built for speed. It was much lighter and there was far less room in it than in any coach in which she had travelled before. She could feel by the way the wheels bounced over the road that the horses found it had little weight to slow them down.

'Did he . . . did he say he was sending me home?' Sheena asked.

'Nay, he didna say that, but where else would we be going?' Maggie asked. 'Nowhere in France is safe for ye, ye can be sure of that.'

Sheena shut her eyes. It was obvious, of course, that he was sending her home and yet she longed to cry out against it. How could she go and leave him behind? How could she bear to go and never see him again?

She thought of his face but somehow she could not make a picture of it. Somewhere stirring in the depths of her memory was something he had said last night. He had been tender—or had she dreamed it? He had spoken words of love. No, indeed, she must have dreamed that.

She could not remember. She could recall quite clearly the terror as she lay helpless and unable to move in the great four-poster bed in the King's bedchamber. And then he had come to rescue her. She could feel again that sudden warmth and the knowledge that her love was flooding over her like a full tide.

He had picked her up in his arms and she had known that she was safe even though she could not speak and could not move. And after that she could remember no more. She forced herself to think back, but somehow it was an utter blank.

'I knew no good would come of this journey,' Maggie was saying. 'Ye're not the type, thank the Lord, who should be living in Palaces with those as has lustful ways and whose wickedness stinks to the very nostrils of Heaven.'

Sheena wanted to smile at Maggie's denunciations but

she could not deny that they were true; no one knew that better than she. They were true. The wickedness and evil was all there and they had tried to make her a part of it.

And yet now the moment was upon her she did not want to leave. She wondered if all her life would be spent dreaming of the Duc, remembering her love for him, remembering and recalling the way in which her heart seemed to leap into her mouth when he appeared, and remembering how she had hated him and not realised all the time that it was because she was so near to love.

The coach came suddenly to a halt. Sheena looked at Maggie and knew that the terror on her face was echoed on her own. Instinctively, without a word, the two women's fingers were interlocked. The coach door was opened. Sheena awaited, tense with every nerve of her body, the command to alight.

Then someone got into the coach and with a feeling of astonished relief she saw who it was.

'Gustave!'

The Christian name came easily to her lips. She forgot to be formal.

'Sheena, thank God you are safe! You were late and I was beginning to worry.'

Unobtrusively Maggie moved from Sheena's side to the small seat with its back to the horses and the Comte sat down beside Sheena and taking her hands in his raised them to his lips.

'Why are you here?' she asked.

'The Duc told me to wait for you,' he said. 'I am to escort you from the environs of Paris to the first stopping place.'

'And then what happens?' Sheena asked, a sudden hope rising in her heart.

'I do not know,' the Comte replied. 'I have just been given my orders.'

'Oh!'

Sheena could not help the note of disappointment sounding in the monosyllable.

'All that matters is that you will be safe,' Gustave said.
Sheena looked him in the eyes.

'How much do you know?' she asked.

'Very little,' he answered. 'Only that the Queen has been up to some of her tricks and that the Duc was able to rescue you in time.'

'Yes, just in time,' Sheena breathed.

'It was not possible to tell more,' Gustave went on. 'there were many things to be arranged. All the Duc wanted was that you should have an escort of someone reliable for the first part of the journey.'

'Where are we going?' Sheena asked.

'Towards the coast,' he said.

'I guessed that,' she replied, and felt again that sudden heaviness because even though she was going home she must leave the Duc behind.

'I am not concerned with anything,' the Comte was saying, 'except that you are safe.'

'I cannot believe what happened last night was true,' Sheena said.

'Who was there?' the Comte asked briefly.

'The Marquess de Maupré.'

'That swine!'

'Why do you say that?' Sheena asked.

'Do you not yet know him for what he is?' the Comte enquired. 'He is one of the lowest beasts that ever stepped this earth. A procurer; a man who makes a living by catering for the depraved taste of those who can afford to pay for it.'

Sheena gave a little exclamation of horror.

'Yes, it is true enough,' he said. 'You may as well know the sort of people from whom the Duc is rescuing you. Maupré started in quite a small way by finding nobles who wanted to be introduced to pretty girls. He made love to them himself and then recommended them to those who could afford to pay what he asked.'

The Comte's tone of voice was a condemnation in itself.

'Then he aimed high and tried to interest the King in his

wares,' he went on, 'but the Duchesse made short shrift of him and so he changed his allegiance and went over to the enemy. He became the Queen's flunkey, someone who was always at her beck and call, someone who was always ready to procure anything that she asked of him.'

Sheena put her hands up to her ears.

'Do not tell me any more,' she begged.

She saw now what a fool she had been to be taken in, as perhaps many other foolish girls had been, by the Marquess's good looks, by his persuasive tongue, by the apparent sincerity of his love-making. And all the time he was trying to inveigle her into being interested in the King simply because the Queen required her, or someone else, to distract His Majesty's attention from the Duchesse whom he adored.

'I am sorry,' the Comte said quietly. 'I should not have spoken so violently. Even the name Maupré makes me see red.'

'You are right, quite right, in all you think about him,' Sheena said. 'Do not let us speak of him any more.'

'Let us speak about ourselves,' Gustave said. 'I understand from the Duc that you are leaving France. Instead, will you not stay with me?'

He spoke with a yearning which seemed to come from the very depth of his being, and then, before Sheena could say anything, he went on:

'I have estates far away in Bordeaux. We could drive there now and no one would be the wiser what had happened to you. We could be married in the chapel which adjoins my château. I am well off, Sheena. I could give you everything you require and I believe that I could make you happy.'

'Thank you, Gustave,' Sheena said tenderly. 'Thank you for your kindness, for loving me and for offering to make me your wife. But I cannot say yes.'

'You will be safe with me,' Gustave insisted.

'It is not my safety which concerns me,' Sheena replied.

'Then what?' he asked.

185

She looked into his eyes and in the pale dawn sunshine coming into the windows it seemed to him that he looked down into the very depth of her soul.

'You are in love with someone else,' he said intuitively. Sheena nodded.

'The lucky devil!' he exclaimed. 'What would I give to stand in his shoes? But I might have known I could never be good enough for you.'

'It is not that,' Sheena said. 'Oh, Gustave, it is not that. You are too good for me, much too good, but I could never marry anyone without love—and as it is I shall never marry!'

'You mean that he does not love you?' Gustave asked. Sheena shook her head.

'There are many, many barriers between us,' she said. As if to comfort her, Gustave kissed her fingers and then held her hand protectively in his as they drove in silence while Maggie fell asleep on the seat opposite them.

There was a long, long day ahead of them and they talked a little and slept a little as the coach carried them swiftly and without incident towards the coast.

It was dark and the horses were picking their way slowly over country roads before they reached the inn where they were to stay the night.

'I shall not see you in the morning,' Gustave said, as, exhausted, Sheena turned towards the stairs.

'You mean you will not be here?' she asked.

'No,' the Comte answered. 'I am to stay an hour or so to see that all is well and then ride back to Paris.'

'But . . . but why?' Sheena questioned.

'My dear, I do not know,' he said. 'But I can only obey orders. You see, as far as I am concerned the Duc commands and I do not question his instructions.'

'Why do you do this for him?' Sheena asked curiously.

'For one reason because he is the finest man I ever met in my life,' the Comte answered. 'For another, because it is too late now for me to recount all his kindnesses to me since I first came to Paris.'

Long after she had said goodbye to the Comte and was lying on her hard bed at the inn Sheena could hear his voice saying: 'He is the finest man I ever met.'

Why had she not realised from the very beginning, she wondered, that the Duc stood head and shou'ders above everyone else in the Palace? Why had she let herself be swept away into an anger and hatred of him merely because she had overheard one cynical remark?

How stupid she had been; how blind! And now it was too late. Tomorrow she would sail away to Scotland and leave him behind. It was then, in the darkness of the room at the inn, that she realised that even her love for her homeland was as nothing beside her love for this strange, unaccountable man who had come into her life.

She had clung to her thoughts of home because they were all she knew of security. Now she saw her existence there for what it was—empty and lonely; her father away in Edinburgh; she and Maggie struggling to make ends meet on a small allowance; the house crumbling into ruins, the gardens unkept and neglected.

What else could she expect while her country was at war? And, because she was only a woman after all, she felt weak and unable to cope with it all.

She must have s'ept for a little while, for she was awoken by Maggie telling her it was five o'clock and the coachmen were ready to be off. They had a hasty breakfast and then were on the road again, travelling at a great speed.

They must have gone for many miles before Sheena dared to ask the question that was in her mind.

'Do you think, Maggie,' she asked tremulously, 'that we shall ever see the Duc de Salvoire again?'

'Nay, there's little sense of it,' Maggie answered. 'He will have made arrangements, I daresay, for our berths aboard a ship. Perhaps the messenger left Paris before we did. But otherwise there's nowt more he can do for us.'

'Nothing more,' Sheena said, and shut her eyes as if she could no longer bear the sunshine outside.

They reached the coast. The sea looked grey and a wind was rising which made Maggie moan at the memory of her last journey through the North Sea. The coach drew up at a small inn and the head coachman climbed from his box to wish Sheena *bon voyage*.

'Thank you for bringing me here so swiftly,' Sheena said, and gave him one of the few gold coins that she and Maggie still possessed.

He thanked her and she watched the horses move away, her eyes lingering on the emblazoned coat-of-arms until she could no longer see it because the tears blinded her.

Maggie had already walked into the small inn. Sheena stood for a moment looking out over the grey sea. It was fitting, she thought, that the sunshine should not be on it, for it seemed to her that her whole life in future would be grey and pointless.

'I must work for Scotland,' she told herself, and wished that the flame of patriotism that had been there in the past could infuse some fire into her words.

She turned away and went into the inn. The innkeeper, bowing politely, met her in the passage.

'The sitting-room reserved for you is at the end of the passage, Ma'mselle,' he said.

'Thank you,' she answered.

She had walked away from him before she remembered it might have been wise to ask him when there was a ship sailing and whether he knew if any reservations had been made for herself and Maggie. And then, because of the unhappiness in her heart, she felt that she could not speak to anyone for the moment.

She wanted to be alone. She wanted to take a hold of her courage which was all she had left with which to face the future. She opened the door of the low-ceilinged room.

There was a bow window looking over the sea and a fire burning brightly in the big open hearth; and because at last she was unobserved, Sheena let the tears roll down her cheeks and as she shut the door she stood for a moment with her back against it, her eyes shut, savouring in its fullness the aching and loneliness of her heart.

'Do you really mind leaving so much?' a voice asked quietly, startling her into giving a gasp as she opened her eyes and saw him standing there at the far side of the room, his hands resting on the back of a high chair.

'You!' she exclaimed. 'I did not expect to find you here.'

'And I did not expect to find you crying,' the Duc answered.

He walked across the room and taking her little chin in his fingers turned her face up to his.

'Why these tears?' he asked. And then as she did not answer but only stared at him, he added gently: 'Is it France that you mind leaving or your little Queen?'

She shook her head dumbly, unable to find her voice, unable, for the moment, to realise that he was really there, and at her side.

'What then?' he insisted.

There was something in his voice, in the expression on his face and the touch of his hands, which made her realise that he knew. She felt the colour rise into her cheeks in a sudden flood, felt herself begin to tremble while her hands crept up to stop the throbbing of her breast.

'Cannot you tell me?' he asked very, very softly.

Again she could not answer; and now suddenly, surprisingly, his arms were around her and his lips were very close to hers.

'I love you, you foolish child,' he said. 'Did you really think I would let you go alone, or that I would ever let you go?'

She felt something leap within her. She felt a sudden quickening over her whole body. Then his lips were on hers and his mouth took her very soul into his keeping.

How long they stood there together she had no idea. She only knew that the whole room seemed to be full of sunshine and the voices of angels. She only knew that from utter despair she had been raised into Heaven itself and that Heaven lay in his lips on hers.

At last they moved apart and he drew her towards the fire so that they sat close together on an old oak settle.

'I had things to attend to in Paris before I dared leave,' he said. 'First amongst them was permission from the King for a new project of mine and his consent to our marriage.'

'His . . . consent!' Sheena could hardly breathe the words.

'Yes, I have it in writing if you disbelieve me,' the Duc answered with a smile. 'But before you give me your promise to be my wife I have something to ask of you.'

Her eyes were almost blinding in their glory as with her lips parted she asked:

'What is it?'

'I want you to come away with me,' he said. Then, seeing the surprise in her face, he went on: 'Yes, really away; not just to Scotland but to the furthermost parts of the earth, for that is where I am going and that is where I will take you as my wife.'

'But, I . . . I do not understand,' Sheena faltered.

'To a new world,' he answered. 'A world which Christopher Columbus has been discovering for Spain; a world in which France already has a small foothold and must gain a great deal more territory.'

'And you are going there?' Sheena exclaimed incredulously.

'I have been meaning to go for a long time,' the Duc replied. 'I am tired of Paris, little Sheena. Like you I have seen the evil, the cruelty and the horror of it. Like you I have seen that many Royal causes are doomed to failure if not disaster.'

He paused for a moment to kiss her hand, turning it over to press his lips into the soft, warm palm.

'Forget all that has happened to you,' he said. 'It is not a life for you or for me. We will find our own world elsewhere.'

'I still do not understand,' Sheena said, although somehow it did not matter.

She was quivering from his kisses, trembling with the excitement that was running through her body, the closeness of his arms and his lips. Whatever he said sounded more wonderful that it was possible to believe. And yet because he expected it of her she knew she must ask questions and listen to his answers.

'For three years now,' the Duc said, 'I have been fitting up a ship, spending some of my own money and some from the Privy Purse. I had the full consent of the King and the Duchesse to make this expenditure on behalf of France. But I also wished to make it on my own account. I want to get away; I want to live a full, man's life without wasting my youth on the frivolities and stupidities of the Court.'

He tightened his arm around her.

'That was why I was at Brest when you arrived in France,' he went on, 'to see how my ship was progressing. And I found it was ready. I went back to the Palace eager for permission to sail.

'Then as the days passed I knew I could not go—unless you would go with me.'

'You wanted me . . . even at the beginning of our acquaintance?' Sheena asked wonderingly.

'I think from the first moment I saw you,' the Duc answered. 'But I was afraid to trust my own senses, my own instincts. I had been let down by women before. I thought they would always be utterly unimportant in my life—until I came to know you.'

'But you were angry with me,' Sheena cried. 'You disapproved of me.'

'I was wildly, crazily jealous,' he answered. 'And as for being angry, it was only because I was so afraid for you. I saw where your steps were leading you. I saw how the Queen, with her diabolical meddling in witchcraft, intended to use you to attract the attention of the King.'

Sheena hid her face against his shoulder at the memory and he kissed her hair.

'The Queen is a little mad, I think, where His Majesty is concerned,' the Duc ruminated. 'Though she is far saner and cleverer in other ways than most people imagine.'

'Why did you not warn me?' Sheena protested.

'Would you have listened?' he asked with a smile.

'I was so stupid,' she said humbly. 'So foolish. And when you did talk to me I defied you merely because . . . because . . .'

'Because what?' the Duc asked tenderly.

'Because I think I was afraid of loving you,' she answered.

He bent his head to find her mouth and once again they were lost in the magic and wonder of the kiss that held them spellbound. And as she surrendered herself utterly to the fire of his passion Sheena felt as if she was already part of him. . . .

A little later, with his arm around her, the Duc led her to the window and they looked out over the sea.

'There is our future beyond the horizon,' he said. 'It may mean hardship and danger; it may mean privation and great difficulties. Are you afraid to face it?'

Even as he spoke the evening sun came through the clouds and lit the sea with a sudden blaze of glory. It was no longer grey, it was blue and emerald, white and silver.

'I will never be afraid as long as I am with you,' Sheena whispered.

The sea was forgotten as his lips searched for hers again and he whispered against them:

'I love you! Oh, little Sheena, I love you more than life itself!'

If you would like a complete list of Arrow books please send a postcard to
P.O. Box 29, Douglas Isle of Man, Great Britain.